Melody
— FOR —
MURDER

A BERTIE BIGELOW MYSTERY

Melody FOR MURDER

CAROLYN MARIE WILKINS

𝓟
Pen-L Publishing
Fayetteville, Arkansas
Pen-L.com

Chapter One

Bertie Bigelow had not had a decent night's sleep in over a week. Since the incident last Saturday, she'd tossed and turned until the wee hours every night, her mind a tumult of doubt and recrimination. As the founder and director of the Metro Community College Choir, Bertie was an old hand at coping with dramatic situations. Tantrums, turmoil, and tears were par for the course in the hours before an important performance. But this year's Christmas concert had been different. Never before had a student taken such flagrant advantage of her trust.

For days after the concert, Bertie refused to set foot on campus. She'd graded her exams at home, steadfastly ignoring the messages piling up in her email inbox. But finally, on the last day of the semester, she had agreed to meet her best friend, Ellen Simpson, in the Starbucks across the street from school.

"In ten years of teaching, I thought I'd seen it all," Bertie said. "I've had gangbangers, thugs, and hustlers in my choir. But none of them has ever pulled a stunt like this—*ever*." She stirred her latte and stared glumly out the window at the students picking their way through the snow and slush on Halsted Street. "I'm lucky I didn't get fired."

Short and soft-spoken, with a full bosom and generous hips, Bertie Bigelow was just shy of forty. With her thin lips and aquiline nose, she liked to think she looked a lot like Lena Horne, if perhaps a bit heavier. As usual, she was impeccably turned out in an elegant, black power suit, her reddish-brown hair straightened to within an inch of its life and cut so that it framed her tan face in perfect symmetry.

"Have you even looked at the video?" Ellen said, reaching across the table to pat her best friend on the arm. "You know how critical you are. I'll bet it wasn't nearly as bad as you think."

Referred to as the Dynamic Duo by their students at Metro Community College, Bertie and Ellen had been friends for nearly ten years. While Bertie was short and round, Ellen Simpson was tall and slender with ebony skin, a raspy voice, and a no-nonsense Afro. As chairman of the English department, Ellen was as well known for her sharp tongue as for the colorful African dresses she wore.

"You're only saying that because you weren't there," Bertie replied, shaking her head mournfully.

"Fat chance," Ellen said tartly. "But until this college recognizes Kwanzaa as an official school holiday, I am boycotting all college-sponsored Christmas celebrations. Whatever this horrible incident was, Professor Bigelow, you're going to have to tell me about it yourself."

"I'm sure it's all over YouTube by now anyway," Bertie said with a sigh.

Located in a squat, concrete fortress at the epicenter of Chicago's impoverished South Side, Metro Community College was the last remaining cultural outlet in this once vibrant area. More than two thousand people had turned out to hear Bertie's choir perform, and the Metro Performance Center had buzzed with anticipation as the evening began.

"Every seat in the house was taken," Bertie continued. "And just in case I wasn't feeling enough pressure, Alderman Clark and Mayor Davis were sitting in the first row next to our beloved Chancellor Grant."

Ellen, an outspoken left-wing activist, pulled a sour face at the mention of Grant's name.

"I can see that pathetic old toady kissing up to those politicians now," she said. Bobbing her head submissively, she continued in an exaggerated Southern dialect. "Metro College is sho 'nuff workin' wonders with dese here underprivileged masses, Mistuh Boss Man. Just lissen to muh little darkies sing."

Bertie giggled. "Don't start with this mess, Ellen. Let me finish telling you what happened." After a week of self-imposed isolation, Bertie was suddenly eager to tell Ellen her version of the story.

"By all means, my dear," Ellen laughed. "Out with it."

As she relived the events leading up to the incident, Bertie felt her stomach tighten. How could she have failed to anticipate such a terrible disaster? As usual, she'd rehearsed the choir right up until the last moment, making sure the performance was as polished as possible. When she'd walked out on to the stage in her favorite evening gown and a pair of four-inch, Italian heels, Bertie had been absolutely certain the evening would be a success.

"Everything was going along perfectly," she said. "The altos were in tune for once. The tenors even remembered their lyrics. Tamara Dupree sang 'O Holy Night' so beautifully that even Old Man Grant was wiping away the tears. And then it happened."

"What happened? Come on, Bertie. The suspense is killing me."

"LaShawn Thomas happened," Bertie said.

Tall and spindly, LaShawn had cornrowed hair, big ears, chocolate colored skin, and an infectious smile. The boy had been Bertie's special project for over a year. For his first six months at Metro, LaShawn barely said a word. But after Bertie had encouraged him to join the choir, he'd blossomed into a star performer. This semester, LaShawn had even made the Dean's List.

Just before LaShawn's number, Bertie introduced the two politicians sitting in the front row to the audience. As the crowd applauded dutifully, Mayor Davis, a stocky white man with a bulbous red nose, grinned genially and waved. Not to be outdone, Alderman Fred Clark, known to his constituents as "Steady Freddy," stood

3

up and blew kisses. Elegantly turned out in a silk shirt and designer suit, Alderman Clark was the epitome of the successful South Side politician—smooth and genial, as long as you stayed on his good side. Now it was time for the grand finale, the showstopper Bertie and her choir had been rehearsing for months.

Hip-hop music began to throb from the sixteen speakers lining the walls of the auditorium. On a screen at the back of the stage, the image of a black Santa waved from the driver's seat of a Hummer H2 convertible. Illuminated in the glare of a single spotlight, LaShawn Thomas danced his way to the microphone at the center of the stage.

"Yo, Englewood, whazzup!" LaShawn shouted, pumping his fists in the air. "Before we go ahead with our final number, I wanna give a shout-out to my man, Alderman Fred Clark. Can I get a spotlight here? That's right. Shine the light on our one and only Steady Freddy Clark—the Voice of Englewood. Did you know he's running for reelection this spring?"

As the white circle of light focused on the Alderman, LaShawn pulled the microphone close to his lips. But instead of singing "'Twas the Night Before Christmas," he began to rap:

> Here in the hood, we think Clark's a saint
> But I wanna tell y'all
> A saint he ain't
> Clark talks all fine
> Like his shit don't stink
> But the man be lyin'
> Lemme tell you what I think
>
> Steady Freddy Clark
> is a butt-kissing flunkie
> A liar, a crook, and a pill-poppin' junkie
> A liar, a crook, and a pill-poppin' junkie.

"I'm standing in the wings watching this and thinking to myself, 'This can't be happening,'" Bertie said. "It's like I was stuck in the middle of one of those 3-D horror movies."

"Bertie, you've got to be kidding me," Ellen said, shaking her head in disbelief. "What happened next?"

"By this point, the entire Performance Center is in an uproar," Bertie continued grimly. "LaShawn is standing in the center of the stage, spewing profanity with a spotlight on his face and a death grip on the microphone. Every other word out of his mouth is the n-word, the f-word, or worse. The students are stamping their feet and hollering. Steady Freddy is shaking his fist and shouting. Mayor Davis looks like he's having a heart attack, and Chancellor Grant is trying to pull himself up over the footlights and onto the stage."

"It's a good thing I wasn't there, Bert. I'd have slapped that boy upside his nappy little head. What on earth was his problem? Do you think he was high or something?"

"Didn't seem like it. When the lights finally came on, LaShawn was standing there with tears running down his face. He ran out the stage door before I could say a word. I haven't heard from him since."

"Bet you've heard from our Fearless Leader, though."

Bertie sighed. "He left a pretty intense message on my cell phone the next day. Lucky for me, he was on his way out of town for the holidays. Otherwise, I'd be sitting in his office getting chewed out this very minute."

"Good thing you've got tenure," Ellen said. "Otherwise, he'd have fired your behind on the spot."

The two women contemplated the gravity of the situation in silence.

"When I got my tenure, Delroy went over my contract with a fine-toothed comb."

Nine months ago, Bertie's husband, Delroy, a brilliant lawyer and the love of her life, had been killed by a hit-and-run driver. She knew she needed to get on with her life, but at times like these, 'getting on' barely seemed worth the effort.

5

"In that case, I wouldn't give Grant and his minions another thought," Ellen said. "Delroy Bigelow was the finest lawyer on the South Side of Chicago. If your husband gave it his seal of approval, I'm sure your contract is unbreakable."

Bertie sniffed and wiped away a tear with the back of her hand.

"Honestly, girl. You're the best friend anyone could ever have."

"So they tell me," Ellen said with a wink. "At the risk of opening up the waterworks again, may I ask what you're doing over the holidays?"

Bertie shrugged and stared down at the unfinished blueberry muffin on her plate.

"What about going out to a party or something? You can't spend the rest of your life in mothballs. If Delroy were here, he'd be the first to tell you not to sit home alone brooding."

"I know," Bertie said with a sigh. "I'm going to my sister Della's in Boston for Christmas, and I've been invited to the Octagon Gala for New Year's Eve, but I don't know if I'll go."

"The Octagon Society? Well, la-di-da." Extending her right pinky, Ellen took a delicate, aristocratic sip from her coffee cup. "They're way too rich for my blood. Even if I could afford to join, I'd be way too dark for those damn-near-white Negroes."

Bertie blushed. "Girl, please. They're not nearly as color struck as they used to be. But it really doesn't matter. I'm probably not going anyway."

"You need to get out and circulate," Ellen said. "Even if it's with those snobby-assed Octagons. Who invited you?"

"Judge Green. He left a message on my voice mail about it last night, but I haven't gotten back to him."

Ellen's eyes widened in surprise. "Theophilous Green? The man's got to be at least a hundred years old. Wears the worst toupee I've ever seen, and I'm not so sure his teeth are real, either."

"He's more like seventy, but you see my problem," Bertie said. "The gala is strictly a couples affair—no unescorted women allowed.

If I want to go to this thing, it's probably Judge Green or no one. But like I told you, I doubt if I'm going to go."

"Nobody is saying you shouldn't go, Bert. The Octagons throw the most extravagant dress ball in all of black Chicago. If I'm not mistaken, the Temptations played there last year."

"It's going to be the Count Basie Orchestra this time," Bertie said. "I haven't seen them since the Count died. Everyone says they're swinging just as hard as ever."

"Promise me you'll think about going," Ellen said. Wiping her mouth with a napkin, she stood up and planted a kiss on Bertie's cheek. "I know Judge Green is a pompous, old fuddy-duddy. And yes, he's almost twice your age. But on the bright side, you'll be catching up with old friends and dancing to the Count Basie Orchestra. What could possibly go wrong?"

Chapter Two

The Museum of Science and Industry had never looked so beautiful. Built to celebrate the Colombian Exposition of 1893, the massive domed structure sat at the northern edge of Jackson Park, overlooking Lake Michigan. A set of graceful neoclassical columns and the wide stone steps at the front of the building gave it an added air of dignity. Mrs. J. D. Leflore, the President of the Octagon Society, stood at the front of the lobby, greeting her guests as they entered. Dressed for this occasion in a floor-length sable coat, Donna Karan gown, and massive diamond necklace, the formidable Mrs. Leflore was considered the Dolly Madison of black Chicago. A nod from her perfectly coiffed head meant instant acceptance into the inner echelons of the city's African American elite. As Judge Green stood next to Bertie at the front of the reception line, she saw the old dowager's eyebrow lift ever so slightly.

"*Delighted* to see you, Mrs. Bigelow." Mrs. Leflore had a well-modulated, stately voice, similar in tone and diction to that of Queen Elizabeth. "And Judge Green. What a pleasure."

"The pleasure is all mine," Theophilous simpered, bending at the waist to plant a kiss on Mrs. Leflore's liver-spotted hand. A small, olive-complected gentleman in his early seventies, the judge was nattily turned out for the big dance in a vintage tuxedo and a maroon bow tie. "This affair is quite the *ne plus ultra*, if I do say so. There is no other event in the city with similar *gravitas*."

As a *magna cum laude* graduate of Harvard Law School (Class of 1961) and the first African American to sit on the Illinois Supreme Court, Green had earned the right to pepper his phrases with legal terminology. Inwardly, Bertie sighed. At this rate, it was going to be a very long evening. The only thing that kept her from running for the nearest exit was her deeply ingrained sense of social propriety and the fact that soon she'd be dancing to the Count Basie Orchestra.

Thronging the lobby were most of black society's movers and shakers—ministers, doctors, and lawyers rubbed shoulders with businessmen and the occasional state senator while their wives, arrayed in designer gowns and sparkling with diamonds, fluttered in attendance. As Bertie and Judge Green wove their way through the crowd, she spotted Alderman "Steady Freddy" Clark standing a few feet ahead of her, chatting up a group of potential campaign donors. After the debacle at the Metro College Christmas Concert, Steady Freddy was the very last person on earth Bertie wished to see. In due course, she intended to apologize humbly and abjectly for LaShawn's bizarre outburst. But tonight she was dressed to the hilt and surrounded by several hundred of Chicago's most successful black folks. It was neither the time nor the place. Hastily, she tugged on the judge's arm and pointed to one of the fifty Christmas trees from around the world that had been set up in the museum's spacious marble lobby. Draped with tinsel and sparkling with colorful decorations, the Guatemalan tree cast a soft glow over the stream of revelers entering the building.

"Look, Theophilous," she said, steering the judge away from the group surrounding the Alderman. "Have you ever seen a lovelier Christmas tree in your life?"

"Top of the line, my dear," Theophilous said. "*Ne plus ultra*, this whole affair. Mrs. Leflore and the rest of the planning committee are to be congratulated." As the judge surveyed the crowd, his expression turned sour.

"I just saw someone I need to talk to," he said. "I'll only be a minute." Without waiting for a reply, he strode away and vanished into the crowd.

As Bertie stood alone and uncertain in the midst of the revelers, a tall man with linebacker's body and a shaved head enveloped her in a bear hug.

"Mac," Bertie said, standing on tiptoe to kiss him on the cheek. "Sure is good to see you."

David Mackenzie and Bertie's late husband, Delroy, had been both colleagues and best friends. Five years ago, Mackenzie had left the Cook County Prosecutor's Office to open his own wildly successful private practice. Despite his impressive credentials, Mac's boundless energy and cheerful demeanor reminded Bertie of an oversized Labrador puppy.

"Where have you been keeping yourself?" Mac asked. "I haven't seen you in months."

Bertie shrugged. "Haven't felt like going out much since the funeral, I guess."

"I know it's tough, Bert, but don't forget your friends. I've missed you." Wrapping his arm around Bertie's shoulders, the lawyer gave her a protective squeeze.

"Back, David, back. Don't crush the woman to death."

Angelique Mackenzie was as tiny and delicate as her husband was massive. Though their social interactions were friendly enough on the surface, Bertie was pretty sure Angelique Mackenzie disliked her intensely. Maybe that was the reason Angie's beaked nose, long fingernails, and elaborate bouffant hairdo made Bertie think of hawks, vultures, and other predatory birds.

"I've been meaning to call you for weeks," Angelique said. "But between the Jack and Jill Charity Fund Drive and taking care of this crazy husband of mine, I haven't had a second to spare."

"That's okay," Bertie said. "Truth is, I haven't been feeling all that social anyhow."

"Hang in there, kiddo," Big Mac said, giving her arm a playful squeeze. "So. Who's the lucky guy who got to be your date for the evening?"

Bertie blushed and looked down. "Theophilous Green brought me," she said. "I don't know if I'd go so far as to call it a date, though."

"I would," Angelique said. "Hope you've been brushing up on your Latin."

"Well, you know how it is," Bertie replied. "If you study hard in school, you never know what heights you may reach—*Labor omnia vincit*, as they say."

"The man's old enough to be your father," Big Mac said. "At least you won't have to worry about him making any sudden moves."

"Not unless I'm prepared to administer CPR afterwards," Bertie grinned. "You haven't seen the good judge lately, have you?"

"As a matter of fact, I have. He's over by the bar talking with Dr. Momolu Taylor. See?"

The doctor was short, his dark skin highlighted by the flowing, purple robe and matching kufi hat he wore. As he stood across from Theophilous Green on the far side of the room, he leaned on a hand-carved ebony walking stick, his head bent to the side, as if listening intently.

"Taylor?" Bertie laughed. "If I was worried about sudden moves, he'd be a man I'd want to keep away from."

Angelique rolled her eyes. "That man is trouble with a capital T. He's got to be pushing fifty, and God knows he's not the best looking man in the room, but he's always got some pretty young thing panting after him."

"It's that sexy African accent of his. He's a distant cousin of some Liberian diamond billionaire. Women circle around him like moths to the flame," Bertie said.

"Delroy did some legal work for Dr. Taylor years ago," Mackenzie said. "I always had the sense your husband hated his guts."

"No surprise there," Angelique said. "Men are animals at heart, you know. Competitive as all get-out. Isn't that right, baby?" She kissed Mac playfully on the cheek. "Rumor has it the doctor's latest conquest is the girl who won the Illinois Idol contest last year. Can you imagine?"

"Patrice Soule? You've got to be kidding me," Bertie said. "She's a terrific singer. Great range and an unusual quality to her upper notes."

"I know you teach singers for a living, but you can spare me the professional assessment," Angelique said. "Something tells me Dr. Momolu Taylor is more interested in her lower parts."

In spite of herself, Bertie burst out laughing. "I suppose I'd better go and rescue him from Theophilous's clutches before he keels over from an overdose of pomposity."

Bertie headed across the lobby toward her date. But as she came closer, she realized that Theophilous and Dr. Taylor were involved in something more than idle chitchat. Though she couldn't make out what was being said, the judge had leaned in close and was poking a bony finger into Taylor's chest for emphasis.

Just as Bertie was about to turn away, the doctor spotted her.

"Come, Bertie. Join us," he said, arranging his face into a welcoming smile. "Theophilous told me you were his date for the evening. You have no idea how jealous I am."

Taking her by the hand, Taylor pulled Bertie close and, holding on to her a full beat longer than the socially accepted norm, brushed his lips slowly across her cheek.

"I shall never forget the work your late husband did for my clinic. He will be greatly missed." The doctor's lyrical African accent turned even the most mundane utterance into music. "If there is ever anything I can do for you, call on me. Any time, eh?" Although his words were conventional enough, the invitation in the doctor's eyes was unmistakable.

My, my, Bertie thought to herself. *Just standing too close to Dr. Momolu Taylor could be hazardous to a lady's virtue.*

Judge Green, his thin lips locked in a tight smile, took hold of Bertie's elbow.

"Doctor, I am adjourning our conversation for the present. If you wish to continue it at a more appropriate time, you know where to find me."

"I'll be in touch, Judge Green," the doctor said smoothly. With a nod to Bertie, he sauntered off in the direction of a voluptuous girl in a formfitting, backless evening gown. Approaching from behind, Taylor ran his hand lightly over her bare back and pulled her close. The high tinkle of the young girl's startled laughter left no doubt that she was indeed Patrice Soule, the 2011 Illinois Idol winner and Chicago's Next New Thing.

"Disgusting," Theophilous Green muttered, though Bertie was pretty sure she detected a note of envy in his voice. "I can't imagine what Miss Soule sees in that man."

"There's just no accounting for taste, Theophilous," Bertie said in as soothing a tone as she could muster. "Especially when it comes to matters of the heart."

As he continued to stare disapprovingly toward the laughing couple, the judge shook his head sadly.

"Miss Soule lives in the apartment next door to me. We are old friends. One could even call us business partners. When her new music video is released, my name will be listed among the producers. Of course, I had to make a sizeable investment in the project, but that's how it's done in show business, or so they tell me."

"She's a terrific performer," Bertie said, smiling inwardly. With the cost of producing an eye-catching music video running in the thousands of dollars, she guessed the besotted old fool had given Soule at least ten grand. On the bright side, Patrice Soule just might be one of the tiny handful of diva wannabes to actually make it to the top.

"I'd hoped Patrice might be willing to accompany me this evening, but she had already made other plans. Not that I am not perfectly thrilled to be here with you, Bertie," the judge added hastily, his wrinkled, beige face flush with embarrassment.

"Why don't we go in the ballroom and see if the band has started playing," Bertie said, tactfully changing the subject. "I'm in the mood to do a little dancing."

Taking the judge by the arm, Bertie walked into the main exposition hall where Count Basie's Orchestra had just begun to play. At one end of the cavernous room, a series of model trains wound their way through an elaborate landscape of hills and valleys. Over their heads, fighter planes from World War I hung suspended from the ceiling. After filling their plates with prime rib and scalloped potatoes from the buffet, Bertie and Theophilous found a table on the edge of the dance floor. To Bertie's ear, the band had never sounded better. The horns were brilliant, the saxes rich and sexy, and the man playing Basie's signature licks on the piano didn't miss a note. After a swinging rendition of "One O'clock Jump," a gray-haired man cradling a trombone in the crook of his arm stepped up to the microphone.

"Ladies and gentlemen, we have a very, very special treat for you this evening. Please give a warm welcome to Chicago's own vocalist extraordinaire, Miss Patrice Soule!"

As the crowd applauded, Patrice Soule stepped onstage and took a bow. Resplendent in a glittering, backless evening gown that complemented her generous build, tawny complexion, and shoulder length curls to perfection, Soule looked like a goddess. But something about the way she clutched at the microphone stand, something in the imploring look she gave the piano player, suggested otherwise.

I bet Soule wasn't planning on performing this evening, Bertie thought to herself. *That's the trouble with being a celebrity. Wherever you go, you're always on display. And wherever you go, your adoring public expects you to perform.*

As the band eased into her song, Soule seemed to gain strength from its melancholy melody. Swaying her hips gently in time to the music, she leaned in close to the microphone and, somewhere between a sigh and a whisper, began to sing "My Funny Valentine."

Years ago, Sarah Vaughan had made this song famous. But as Soule's voice floated high and free over the top of the band, it was clear that the 2011 Illinois Idol winner had something of her own to say. But just as the song was about to reach the peak of its emotional journey, Soule's voice faltered. It was a tiny slip—a wobble on the G above middle C, undetectable to all but the most discerning of listeners. But Bertie Bigelow taught singers for a living. To her, the warning signs were clear. If Soule didn't make some fundamental changes to her vocal technique, she would lose her beautiful voice within the year. When Soule had finished, the crowd clapped and shouted their approval.

"Brava, bravissima," Judge Green shouted, his watery hazel eyes sparkling with excitement. "A most spectacular performance. *Ne plus ultra*, wouldn't you agree, Bertie?"

As Bertie contemplated her reply, Charley Howard, a blue-black mountain of a man with a pugnacious jaw and a massive potbelly, approached their table. Ten years ago, Howard had quit his job as a forklift operator and started a business selling his wife's homemade piccalilli over the Internet. Today, aided in part by his close friendship with reputed crime boss Tony Roselli, Charley Howard's Hot Stuff Inc. was the tenth largest condiment company in America. For the past six months, Howard had been trying to penetrate the inner circle of Chicago's African American elite. Despite never having attended college, he'd gotten himself accepted into the Kappa Alpha Psi fraternity and had even wangled an invitation to join the Boulé, the exclusive fraternity of African American overachievers. More than anything, however, Charley Howard wanted to join the Octagon Society.

"Ev'nin', folks," Howard drawled. "Y'all enjoyin' the party tonight?"

"Very much," Bertie said with a smile. "Though I did think the prime rib could have used a touch of Heavenly Hot Stuff to jazz it up a little."

Charley Howard's raucous laughter was loud enough to turn heads at the surrounding tables.

"You got that right! Think I'll pay those white boys back in the kitchen a visit—set 'em straight 'bout who they be dealin' with here."

Theophilous wrinkled his nose as though a mound of excrement had suddenly materialized in his martini.

"With *whom*, Mr. Howard. Set them straight about the people *with whom* they are dealing."

Momentarily confused, Howard looked to Bertie for clarification.

"Don't mind Theophilous," she said with an embarrassed smile. "He's a bit of a stickler when it comes to grammar."

"I'll be the first to admit I ain't much of an expert when it comes to stuff like that," the Hot Sauce King said with a smile.

"*Ignorantia neminem excusat,*" Theophilous muttered, half under his breath.

"Say what?" Charley Howard shrugged affably. "Never mind. Look here, Judge. My application for the Octagon Society has been under consideration since July. Since you're on the membership committee, I was hopin' perhaps you could give things a little push. You know, put in a word to Mrs. Leflore on my behalf?"

"Absolutely not, Mr. Howard," Theophilous said, his hands folded primly in his lap. "The Octagon Society has very strict criteria for membership."

Undeterred, the Hot Sauce King turned to Bertie and winked slyly.

"Oh, I get it. I'm a big boy, Judge. Just tell me how much it's going to take. Ten grand? Fifteen? How about this: Once I become a member, I'll make a twenty thousand dollar donation to the Octagon Scholarship Fund."

Theophilous Green's entire body quivered with indignation.

"That kind of crude influence peddling may be the rule of law in your line of business, but it is entirely inappropriate here. As I just told you, the Octagon Society has *standards*."

"Standards, my black ass," Charley Howard replied. "My hard-earned money's not good enough for you? Just who the hell do you think you are, talkin' to me like that?"

Theophilous laughed—a dry, sandpapery cackle that took both Bertie and the Hot Sauce King by surprise.

"An Illinois Supreme Court Justice, Mr. Howard. I have spent much of my life mediating disputes of a sordid nature. I have absolutely no intention of spending my free time socializing with criminals."

For a minute, Bertie thought the Hot Sauce King was about to explode.

"Don't mess with me, Green," he hissed. "I'm gonna join this goddamn club, whether you like it or not."

"You will do so over my dead body," Theophilous snapped. With a curt nod, the judge stood up and clasped Bertie by the elbow. "Shall we have a dance, my dear?"

Embarrassed by the judge's rudeness, Bertie shrugged helplessly and followed Theophilous onto the dance floor. She looked back over her shoulder to see Charley Howard still standing in front of their table, a look of naked hatred darkening his face.

"Was it really necessary to bait the man like that, Theophilous? He seems nice enough, and Lord knows the scholarship fund could use some extra money."

"I don't care how much money he's got. The man's a pretender—a parvenu who can't even put a proper sentence together."

Bertie cringed inwardly. A *parvenu*? Who said things like that anymore? It was the twenty-first century, for crying out loud. If it hadn't been for the Count Basie Orchestra, she'd have walked off the dance floor in a heartbeat. But at that very moment the drums were pounding, the trumpets were screeching, and her feet had developed an irresistible urge to move to the beat.

For the next few hours, Bertie forgot her troubles and let the music carry her away. Theophilous turned out to be a surprisingly good dancer, in spite of his stuffy manner. When the band launched into "Auld Lang Syne" three hours later, she had to admit she was sorry to see the evening come to an end. She and the judge toasted in the New Year with a glass of vintage Champagne. Maybe it was the music—

the thrill of dancing to such a good band—but in that moment, Bertie felt herself suffused with a rosy glow of pleasure she had not felt since before her husband, Delroy, had died.

"Would you like to come up to my apartment for a brandy?" Having fetched Bertie's mink from the hatcheck girl, Theophilous held it for her gallantly as he spoke. "It is the New Year, after all."

Bertie replied with as much tact as she could muster. "I'm still trying to get my bearings, Theophilous. I'm not ready to be anything more than friends with any man yet."

The judge pulled himself erect. "Of course, my dear, of course. Nothing untoward, I assure you. I was simply inviting you out of friendship."

An awkward silence followed as the couple stepped into the elevator that led to the basement parking garage. *It was stupid to let the judge drive me to the dance*, Bertie thought. *If I'd driven my own car, I wouldn't be stuck in this awkward situation.*

"I hold your late husband in the highest esteem," the judge continued, waving imperiously to summon the parking attendant. "Would you reconsider if I told you I had some papers Delroy left in my care?"

"What kind of papers? Delroy never mentioned he'd left anything with you."

"If you'll do me the honor of gracing my humble abode with the briefest of visits, I'll be happy to show the documents to you."

As the judge's black Lincoln Town Car glided up to the curb in front of them, he opened the passenger door with a flourish and gestured for Bertie to climb in.

"My building is just around the corner. Just a quick stop, and then I'll take you right home."

Chapter Three

TUESDAY, JANUARY 1, 2013—12:30 A.M.

As the elevator whisked her up to the judge's apartment, Bertie began to have second thoughts. All of this was so unfamiliar—uncharted territory, really. It had been more than ten years since she'd been alone with a man in his apartment. In the fall of 2000, she'd spent the night with a handsome lawyer named Delroy Bigelow. Despite the fact that he was fifteen years her senior, Bertie had known the minute she kissed him that Delroy was the man for her. The rest had been history. Ten years of the best marriage any woman could hope for. Of course, all that was over now. Nine months ago, as Delroy was on his way to work, some drunk had run a stop sign and hit him head on. Two hours later, he was dead.

Placing a protective hand under Bertie's elbow, Theophilous guided her off the elevator and unlocked the door to his apartment.

"Here we are," he said. "*Chez moi*, as the French say."

With its plush shag carpet, leather couch, and track lighting, the place reminded Bertie of the kind of bachelor pad James Bond might have brought a lady home to in the 1960s. A small bar, complete with a Pernod sign, a mirror, and two bar stools, stood against the wall. Tasteful paintings of voluptuous black women in various states of undress decorated the wall on the opposite side of the room. From the large picture window on the far wall, Bertie could see the lights of the Museum of Science and Industry twinkling on the other side of Jackson Park.

After hanging his own coat and Bertie's mink in the closet by the door, the judge went to the bar and poured himself a glass of whiskey.

"Can I offer you a libation of some kind? A martini or a glass of sherry, perhaps?"

"No, nothing for me, Theophilous. I've had enough Champagne to last me till next year. You said you had something you wanted to show me? Something that belonged to Delroy?"

"Yes, as a matter of fact, I do. Have a seat, my dear. I'll just be a moment." Setting his whiskey glass on the coffee table, the judge glided across the shag carpet into what Bertie presumed was his bedroom and closed the door softly behind him.

Torn between curiosity and the increasing suspicion that she should never have come here in the first place, Bertie perched gingerly at the end of the black leather couch. Positioned on the wall across from her was the largest flat-screen TV she had ever seen. Five minutes later, Theophilous Green emerged from his bedroom wearing a maroon smoking jacket and looking remarkably like a wizened, café au lait Rex Harrison.

"Your late husband was working on a memoir when he died. A behind-the-scenes look at some of his most famous cases—you know the sort of thing," Theophilous said. "There are lots of well-known Chicagoans in this manuscript. Delroy asked me to read it through to see whether there was anything in it he might get sued for writing about."

Theophilous produced a slim leather briefcase from behind his back and waved it in front of her. But when she reached out her hand, he snatched it away, giggling coyly.

"Oh, no, my dear Bertie. Not so fast. Are you sure I can't offer you a martini? Before I give you this, I thought we could play a little game." Judge Green walked back to the bar, set down Delroy's briefcase, and poured himself another shot of whiskey.

"Look, Theophilous. It's really late. Maybe we should just do this another time," Bertie said.

Instead of replying, he polished off his drink, reached behind the bar, and flipped a switch. Every light in the room went out. With an eerie, mechanical whir, a set of blackout curtains lowered themselves over the living room window, plunging the apartment into total darkness. Suddenly, the massive TV in front of them sprang to life. While soft music thumped suggestively in the background, vivid larger-than-life images of people having sex writhed on the screen in front of her. Before Bertie could fully register this remarkable turn of events, Theophilous was pressing up next to her on the couch, working his liver-spotted hand up her left thigh.

"What on earth has gotten into you?" Bertie said. She stood up and brushed the judge's hand away. "Give me that manuscript and take me home this instant."

Stepping around the coffee table, Bertie strode toward the bar where she'd last seen Delroy's briefcase. Except for the pornographic images flickering across the screen, the room was completely black. In the darkness, she stumbled and fell over what felt like a large leather ottoman. Before she could right herself, the judge was kneeling next to her and pawing at the front of her dress.

"Come on, you saucy little thing," he whispered, his breath hot in her ear. "You know you want me to give it to you."

"Take your hands off me, you pervert! *Now*. Or I will scream."

Judge Theophilous Avery Green cackled smugly and licked Bertie's cheek.

"*Mea culpa*, my dear. I am guilty as charged. I can assure you it will do no good to remonstrate. This room is entirely soundproof." With a surprisingly firm grip, Theophilous pinned Bertie on her side with one arm behind her back. Panting heavily, he pulled up her dress. As he shoved his right hand between her legs, Bertie twisted onto her back and drove her knee straight into his crotch.

Winded and trembling, she staggered to her feet and smoothed down her dress. She'd practiced kicking things as a part of her daily Tae Bo kickboxing workout for years. Who'd have ever thought she'd actually have to kick someone for real? As the judge twisted and turned on the carpet, clutching his privates and moaning softly, Bertie felt her way to the bar and flipped on the lights.

"You should be ashamed of yourself," she said, poking the judge in the side with her toe. Tomorrow morning, I'm reporting your disgusting behavior to the Octagon Society." Bertie took Delroy's briefcase off the bar and stuck it under her arm. "Good night, Theophilous. I'll be taking Delroy's manuscript home now."

Judge Green, his eyes glassy with pain, whimpered softly.

"Don't bother," Bertie said. "I'll see myself out."

The lobby was deserted when Bertie emerged from the elevator. It was well past midnight, and the doorman had retreated to his office in the back to watch TV. No one saw Bertie step out of the elevator and stand in front of the double doors leading to the street. No one saw that her once immaculate ball gown had been ripped near the right breast. No one saw that her hair was a mess or that her makeup was smeared. And no one saw that she was crying.

She sat down on a small leather couch that had been placed next to a giant potted palm for the convenience of visitors. Fishing a tissue from her purse, Bertie dried her eyes and scrubbed the makeup off her face. Then, with shaking hands, she dug out her cell phone and called Yellow Cab. When the taxi arrived moments later, Bertie wrapped her mink coat tightly around her, pulled open the passenger door, and collapsed onto the back seat.

"We are going to Fifty-Seventh and Harper," she told the driver. "I'll direct you from there."

Just as the cab began to pull away, Bertie spotted a familiar figure approaching the building. Although she hadn't seen him since the Christmas concert, Bertie recognized LaShawn Thomas instantly. Dressed in a Chicago Bulls jacket and a pair of unlaced Nikes, her one-time favorite student flung open the ornate double doors of the Jackson Towers Apartments and rushed inside. A small black messenger bag, its flap partially open, dangled from his left shoulder.

Wonder what he's doing here, Bertie thought to herself. Not that she really cared. She slumped down against the cool leather of the taxi's spacious back seat and tried not to cry. Only last week, LaShawn's disruptive behavior had been her biggest concern. But things were different now. Tonight Bertie had learned that the world is a dark and evil place—a place where even trusted friends could turn out to be predators. As her taxi hurtled through the dark and deserted city streets, Bertie vowed to be more discriminating about the kind of people she let into her life.

At that moment, no amount of positive thinking could alter the fact that, after ten years of marriage, Bertie Bigelow was once again a single woman—a vulnerable target for horny and perverted creeps with only her wits and the good Lord to guide her.

The moment she'd locked her front door, Bertie stripped off her battered evening gown and dumped it in the trash. The dress had cost her a small fortune, but she would never be able to wear it again. Dumping a box of Epsom salts and an entire bottle of Savon de Marseille liquid soap into the tub, Bertie spent the next hour scrubbing herself in the scalding, soapy water until her skin was raw.

Chapter Four

Bertie Bigelow tossed and turned most of the night. In her dreams, she ran screaming through the Museum of Science and Industry, followed by Theophilous Green, his black judge's robe flapping open to reveal scrawny, tan legs and an erect penis. As the first wintry sun of 2013 began to peek through her window, she abandoned all hope of getting a decent night's sleep and climbed out of bed. She padded into her kitchen, filled a battered kettle with water, and set it to boil on the stove. It was the start of a brand-new day at the start of a brand-new year. Determined to put the previous night's ordeal as far from her mind as possible, she dug through the basket of magazines she kept next to her kitchen table and extracted the latest issue of *Jet* from the pile.

Blowing on the potent cup of double strength Irish breakfast tea that always jump-started her morning, Bertie leafed through the glossy pictures of movie stars, divas, and wannabes until an article entitled "Beauty of the Week Shares Fitness Tips" caught her eye. Patrice Soule, dressed in a skimpy leopard skin bikini that barely concealed her generous curves, gazed eagerly into the camera. Apparently, in addition to running three miles a day, Soule maintained a nine hundred calorie a day diet and met with her personal trainer daily.

"I like my fried chicken and biscuits as much as anyone," she told her interviewer. "But if I want to rise to the top in this business, I have to keep my figure in top physical shape." In spite of her come-hither beauty and her remarkable voice, Soule struck Bertie as insecure, perhaps even frightened. "You never know how things will turn out in the music business," Soule said. "If I don't stay on my toes, I could lose everything."

Bertie was paging through a delicious, gossipy feature on Beyoncé when her doorbell rang. Wondering who could be bothering her so early on New Year's Day, she pulled a bathrobe over her pink cotton nightie, walked down the short flight of steps that led from the kitchen to her front door, and squinted through the peephole. A dark-haired white man smoking a cigarette stood on her front porch. Between puffs, the man stomped his feet and flapped his arms to keep warm.

"Sorry, Mister," Bertie mumbled under her breath as she turned away from the door. "There is no way I am opening this door to a strange man. Not for all the tea in China. Not after what I've been through."

As Bertie headed up the stairs, her doorbell rang again in a series of staccato bursts. She walked back down the stairs and looked through the peephole again.

"Chicago Police Department, Mrs. Bigelow," the man hollered and banged on the door with his fist.

"Hold up your badge where I can see it," Bertie said. After peering suspiciously at the man's gold shield for several minutes, she shot back the deadbolt and opened the door. A blast of bitter winter air and the smell of tobacco accompanied the policeman inside.

"Detective Michael Kulicki, homicide division," the man said, extending a hand the color and temperature of a large frozen haddock. "I need to ask you some questions."

Tall and stoop-shouldered with thinning gray hair, Kulicki spoke in the flat nasal accent of Chicago's ethnic working class. Instinctively, Bertie's stomach tightened with fear. As a black kid growing up on the South Side of Chicago, she'd watched cops just like this one harass the boys in her neighborhood—forcing innocent kids face down on the pavement to be humiliated and occasionally beaten. Bertie took a deep breath to steady herself. Just because the guy was white and a policeman didn't necessarily make him a racist. Could be that the man, whose bleary eyes and day-old beard indicated he'd gone at least one night without sleep, was just trying to do his job.

"Sorry to keep you waiting," Bertie said. "These days a woman alone can't be too careful. Can I offer you a cup of tea?"

"No thanks, ma'am," Kulicki said, rubbing his hands together. He followed her up to the kitchen and sat down at the table. As Bertie stood silent and wary, Kulicki reached into his back pocket and brought out a small notepad and a pen. "I won't take much of your time. Tell me about your whereabouts last night."

"May I ask why you need to know?" Although Bertie had never studied law herself, she'd often heard Delroy caution his clients never to volunteer more information than absolutely necessary.

"I can have a warrant issued to bring you down to the station. It'll be much easier if you just tell me what you did last night."

In the clipped tone she used to deal with unpleasant authority figures, Bertie gave the policeman an abbreviated account of her activities.

"Are you sure about the time you left the judge, Mrs. Bigelow?"

"Pretty sure. I took a taxi home. You can check the records," Bertie said. "Why all these questions, Detective? What's this all about?"

"Judge Green was found dead in his home this morning," Kulicki said. "Are you sure he was alive when you left his apartment?"

Bertie inhaled sharply. Theophilous had been crawling on the ground, whimpering in pain, but he was definitely alive when she'd left. Surely people don't die from being kicked in the groin, do they?

"What happened, Detective? Did the judge have a heart attack or something?"

The detective's nasal voice was flat, expressionless.

"He was shot in the face with a 9 millimeter handgun at point-blank range."

Bertie felt the room around her begin to spin. Surely, this had to be some kind of bizarre fantasy. Perhaps she was still in bed, dreaming. Placing both hands on the kitchen countertop to steady herself, she repeated Kulicki's words mindlessly.

"Shot? In the face? Who would do such a terrible thing?"

"That's what we're trying to find out, Mrs. Bigelow. The judge was found by his cleaning woman early this morning. He was lying in a pool of blood on the living room floor. The place had been ransacked, and his wallet, laptop, and credit cards are missing. However, the apartment shows no signs of forced entry. It would appear that Judge Green let the killer into the apartment. Do you own a gun?"

"Yes, I suppose I do." Over her strenuous objection, Delroy had insisted on keeping a loaded gun in the bottom drawer of their bedroom dresser. Bertie had always hated the thing, but that didn't change the fact that it was her gun now.

Kulicki's gaze narrowed. "May I see it? You can say no, of course, but I remind you this is a murder investigation. If I have to get a warrant, I'll be back with a team of officers later this afternoon, and we will turn this place inside out. We might need to cut open the cushions of your couch or poke a few holes in your walls to make sure nothing's hidden there. Do you understand me?"

Wordlessly, Bertie climbed the two flights up to her bedroom, fetched the shoebox containing Delroy's Smith & Wesson, and handed it over.

"Thank you for cooperating, Mrs. Bigelow." Kulicki stuck the shoebox under his arm without opening it and stood up. "I'll be in touch."

Judge Green's murder led the evening news that night. While the mayor, the chief justice of the Illinois Supreme Court, and every alderman on the city council expressed their shock and outrage, Police Commissioner James Bailey, looking overwhelmed and exhausted, fended off a barrage of questions. Did the police have a suspect in custody? "No." Did the police have any potential leads in the case? "No." Had the police found the murder weapon? "No." Did the police have any clue as to the identity of the woman who had accompanied Judge Green to his apartment on the night of the murder? Commissioner Bailey's tired blue eyes looked straight into the camera as he announced that yes, a Mrs. Alberta Bigelow had been with the judge on the night he was killed.

Bertie stared in stunned disbelief. As her heart thumped frantically in her chest, her mind spun like a hamster on a wheel. This just could not be happening. Millions of Chicagoans now associated her with the murder. What would her friends say? What about Chancellor Grant and her colleagues at Metro College? Never in all her life had she felt so embattled and alone.

For the next three days, Bertie's phone rang off the hook. Friends called to see if she was alright. Acquaintances called out of morbid curiosity, and people who disliked Bertie called just to hear her admit that yes, she'd actually been desperate enough to go on a date with Theophilous Green. Each person she talked to had a theory about the identity of the murderer. Many people thought Judge Green's murder was just the latest in a series of deadly home invasions taking place on the South Side. Others speculated that the judge had been killed in retaliation. In his forty years on the bench, Judge Green had sent many a man to prison, including members of the Roselli crime family. Perhaps the murderer was someone from Theophilous's past.

No one was rude enough to suggest outright that Bertie, the last person known to have seen the judge alive, could possibly be the murderer. At least, not to her face. Behind her back, Bertie was sure the rumor mill was running overtime.

After dealing with all the gossips and busybodies, David Mackenzie's phone call was a welcome relief.

"I've been worried about you," he said. "Next time the police come by your house, call me, okay? You shouldn't have given the police Delroy's gun."

"It was seven o'clock in the morning on New Year's Day. Even if I'd had the presence of mind to think of calling a lawyer, I wouldn't have wanted to bother you."

"Don't be silly, Bertie. That's what friends are for. You sure your gun hasn't been fired recently?"

"I hate guns," Bertie replied. "I haven't opened that shoebox in years."

"You and I know that's true, but once the police get involved in a situation like this, there's no telling where it could lead. Did you at least get a receipt for the gun?"

"I should have, but honestly, I was so flustered I just handed it over."

Mackenzie grunted. "This is why you need me to look after you. Next time the police call, do not say a word without talking to me." He sighed, then said softly, "You're one of my favorite people, Bertie. I'd hate to see you wind up in jail."

The next day over lunch at Giordano's, a popular pizza parlor located near the University of Chicago's South Side campus, Bertie told Ellen Simpson about her visit to Judge Green's apartment.

Resplendent in a brilliant purple caftan, matching headscarf, and oversized hoop earrings, Ellen shook her head in disgust.

"I'd have shot his sorry, yellow behind for sure," she said. "You sure you didn't kill him, Bertie?"

"Quite sure. As I walked out the door, he was holding his crotch and making whimpering noises. Someone must have shot him after I left."

"I wonder what for," Ellen said. "Other than being a pompous ass and a dirty old man, the guy seemed harmless enough."

"I don't know about that," Bertie said slowly. "Theophilous was a big snob and wasn't shy about telling people he thought he was better than they were. He had a big argument with Charley Howard while we were at the party. I didn't think about it too much at the time, but now I wonder."

"The Hot Sauce King? That man is downright scary. Everybody knows he's in tight with the Roselli Family."

"On the night he was killed, Theophilous called Howard an ignoramus in front of hundreds of witnesses. You think I should have told the police about it?"

"Probably," Ellen said. "When that cop comes by to return your gun, you can tell him."

"*If* they return it."

"They'd better. If they don't, you can ask David Mackenzie to sue their asses for harassment."

"He says I should never have given the police my gun in the first place."

Ellen gave Bertie a speculative look. "You know the man is sweet on you, right?"

"No way. Mac is an old family friend. He's just trying to help me out, that's all."

"For a so-called intelligent woman, you can be really dense, Bertie. Haven't you ever noticed the way he looks at you? That snippy little wife of his sure has."

"There's never been anything between us, and there never will be. The man is *married*, for Pete's sake."

Ellen arched an eyebrow. "Sure he is, honey. Not that it matters all that much."

"Hush your mouth," Bertie said with a nervous giggle. "Now that Delroy is gone, I don't think I'll ever love another man again."

"I know you're still missing Delroy," Ellen said, giving Bertie's arm a sympathetic squeeze. "But sooner or later you need to get back in circulation. And when you do, I think a certain 'family friend' might be interested in more than friendship, if you get my drift."

Bertie blushed beet red. "That does it," she said firmly. "I'm not going to talk about this any more." She took a sip of Merlot and fiddled absentmindedly with her fork.

"Tell you something else I'm curious about. I didn't say anything to the police about this, but the night Theophilous was killed, I saw LaShawn Thomas going into his apartment building."

"Jackson Towers is way out of his income bracket," Ellen said. "I wonder what he was doing there."

"I've been thinking about that," Bertie said. "Since he ruined my Christmas concert, I haven't heard a word from him. No explanation, no apology, nothing. I sure hope he didn't have anything to do with this murder business. You think I should have told that detective about seeing him?"

Ellen shook her head. "No way. You know how the cops are when it comes to our young men. They'll lock his ass up and throw away the key on general principle."

"But what if LaShawn really is a murderer?"

"Girl, please. Clearly, the boy has got some issues. But he's not the kind of kid who would do something like this."

"True," Bertie said slowly. "Then again, I would never have thought he'd go crazy in the middle of the Christmas concert either. Maybe I'm not as good a judge of character as I thought I was."

"You should call his grandmother. LaShawn and his sister have been living there since his father got himself killed trying to rob a liquor store last year."

"What about his mother?"

"Also dead. AIDS, I believe. The kid's come up the hard way, Bertie. His grandmother is the only stable thing in his life. If anyone knows what's going on inside LaShawn's mixed-up little head, Mrs. Petty would. You need to give her a call."

Bertie shook her head. "LaShawn's the one who should reach out to me, not the other way round. Yelling and screaming about Alderman Clark like that. The little brat very nearly got me fired. That is, if I don't get arrested for murder first."

Ellen tipped back her head and laughed. "Girl, please! You're not going to get fired, and you're not going to be arrested, either. I don't disagree that LaShawn is way overdue for an ass-whuppin', but at some level, he's still your student. You need to find out what made him lose it like that."

As usual, Ellen was right.

"I have Mrs. Petty's number and address in my emergency contact files," Bertie said. "I suppose I could at least talk to her."

Chapter Five

LaShawn answered the phone when Bertie called his grandmother's house the next morning.

"Don't even think about hanging up," she said. "I'm coming right over. We need to talk."

On an average day, it took twenty minutes to drive from Bertie's house to the West Englewood neighborhood where Mrs. Petty lived. But today was not an average day. Bertie had done her best to help LaShawn Thomas succeed in life. In return, the boy had embarrassed her in front of her boss, her colleagues, and her students. As she sped west across Garfield Boulevard, she looked forward, with grim pleasure, to confronting the boy face to face.

Fifteen minutes later, Bertie Bigelow pulled to the curb in front of 6729 Paulina Street. In a neighborhood that had clearly seen better days, Mrs. Petty's well-kept, brick bungalow stood out like a beacon of hope. A brightly lit Christmas tree shone through the iron burglar bars covering the downstairs windows, and a small wreath had been hung inside the heavy security gate protecting Mrs. Petty's front door.

She ran up front steps and jabbed her finger impatiently at the doorbell. After several minutes, a small boy opened the door.

"LaShawn's not here," he said.

"Are you sure? I spoke to him on the telephone not twenty minutes ago."

Dressed in pajama pants and a sleeveless undershirt, the boy looked to be around seven years old. In response to Bertie's question, he stuck a grape lollipop in his mouth and stared silently.

"Is Mrs. Petty at home?"

"Grandma's at work. LaShawn's s'posed to babysit, but he ain't here, neither."

"My name is Mrs. Bigelow. I'm LaShawn's music teacher. Do you mind if I wait for him a little while?"

"You must be the choir lady." The boy giggled mischievously, opening the security gate to let her in. "LaShawn tole me you *real* mad at him. He gonna get a whuppin'?"

"I just want to talk to him," Bertie said with a grim smile.

"Oh." The boy looked disappointed, then brightened suddenly. "My name's Benny," he said, extending a small grimy hand. "Wanna see my new KittyKat piano?"

Without waiting for an answer, the boy turned and ran down a long hallway. Bertie sighed, shut the front door, and followed him into the kitchen. A stack of dirty dishes waited on the sideboard next to the sink, and the odor of stale bacon grease hung in the air. Climbing onto one of the three mismatched plastic chairs arranged around the kitchen table, Benny pushed aside a half-eaten bowl of Lucky Charms and pulled out a toy piano shaped like a grinning Cheshire Cat. Placing his lollipop carefully to one side, he poked the instrument with sticky fingers. As if by magic, the device sprang to life, producing an elaborate version of "Old MacDonald Had a Farm," complete with strings and a hip-hop drum beat. With a shout of joy, Benny jumped off the chair and began to improvise a harmony part.

As the boy continued to sing in a clear, pitch-perfect voice, Bertie could not help but smile. LaShawn's disappearing act had put her in a foul mood, but the music teacher in Bertie was intrigued.

"Let's play a game," she said. "I'll play a song, and then you sing it, okay?"

Sure enough, Benny imitated each melody perfectly on the first repetition. Every time Bertie tried to stop, he begged her to play "just one more, *please*." Finally, after Bertie was able to stump him with an intricate tune she was not sure she would have been able to sing back herself, she said, "You know, you're a very good singer, young man."

The boy's chubby brown face glowed with pride. "I love the singing game. LaShawn plays it with me all the time. Please don't be mad at him, Miz Bigelow."

Bertie smiled. The kid's impish charm was hard to resist.

"You're worried about your big brother?"

"LaShawn ain't my brother. He's my uncle." The boy frowned and sucked his lollipop thoughtfully. "What LaShawn do, Miz Bigelow? The man that came yesterday was mad at him, too."

"What man?" Bertie asked sharply.

"The man in the fancy, black coat," Benny said. "He wasn't nice, like you. When I tried to touch his coat, he yelled at me. Said my hands were dirty."

"Did the man tell you his name?"

Benny shook his head. "Nah. He waited around for a while, but when LaShawn didn't come back, he left."

"Is LaShawn hiding in the house somewhere, Benny? If you know where he is, you need to tell me. It's really important."

Benny giggled. "The fancy coat man said the same thing, only he was even madder than you."

Bertie shook her head in frustration. "This is no laughing matter, Benny. Didn't your Mama tell you not to open the door to strangers?"

The boy looked sheepishly at the floor.

"What if a bad person came in? You could get hurt."

"Already got a whuppin' for it," Benny said, rubbing his behind. "But if I didn't let you in, we wouldn't have played the singing game. Can we play some more? Please?"

"One more round, then I've got to go. When LaShawn gets home, tell him to call me right away."

For the rest of the weekend, Bertie's thoughts chased themselves in futile circles. A month ago, she would have said she knew LaShawn Thomas well. She would have said the boy was blessed with a quick mind, a winning personality, and an abundance of musical talent. In May, he would have graduated from Metro College with honors. Instead, the boy had totaled his entire academic career with one grand and utterly inexplicable gesture.

What's more, LaShawn Thomas was now in hiding—not only from Bertie, but from some guy wearing a fancy, black coat. Who was this man? Why was he angry? Did it have anything to do with Judge Green's murder? What had LaShawn been doing in the judge's building, anyway? Bertie sighed. All this solitary speculation was beginning to give her a headache. Fortunately, Ellen Simpson was home when she called Sunday evening.

"After all I've done for that kid, Ellen. I've written recommendation letters, given him hours of extra vocal coaching for free. I even helped him find an afterschool job. Now he won't even talk to me."

Ellen grunted. "I better not run into LaShawn on campus. Might forget myself and slap the boy silly. Did you talk to his grandmother?"

"No. She was at work. I did get to hang out with a delightful seven-year-old, though."

"LaShawn left a seven-year-old kid alone in the house?"

"My guess is he was watching the house from somewhere nearby—a car or perhaps a neighbor's house. He probably returned home the minute I drove away." Bertie sighed. "The boy's in real trouble, Ellen. Someone else is looking for him, too. A man in an expensive, black coat."

"Any idea why?"

"None whatever," Bertie said. "Do you think it might have something to do with the judge's murder?"

"I sincerely hope not. My best advice is to try his grandmother again. You can't beat him. I can't beat him, either. But she can."

"I don't know if a beating is going solve anything at this point," Bertie said, "but I'll try calling Mrs. Petty again in a day or so."

"While I'm on a roll here, let me tell you something else you need to check into," Ellen said. "Do you know what was in that briefcase Theophilous gave you?"

"A manuscript," Bertie said. "Apparently, Delroy was writing a book. Late at night, he'd lock himself away in the den for hours. When I asked what he was working on, he said it was a surprise. That I'd know when the time was right."

"Sounds just like a writer," Ellen said. "When I'm working on a poem, I can stay by myself for days. Aren't you dying to read it?"

"Not really," Bertie said slowly. "Opening that briefcase is going to remind me all over again that Delroy is gone. That he's never ever coming back."

"Come on, Bert. Aren't you even a little curious to read what he wrote?"

"Maybe a little."

"Curiosity is good, Bert. Delroy thought that whatever was in there was important enough for Judge Green to take a look. That should tell you something right there."

Chapter Six

In all the excitement following Judge Green's murder, Delroy's briefcase had lain, forgotten, on the small chest of drawers by the front door. Slim and elegant, it was made of Italian leather and looked expensive—not at all like the squat, sturdy bag Bertie's husband had used to haul his papers back and forth from the office. When had he purchased the thing, and why? That evening, armed with a tall glass of merlot and a box of chocolates, Bertie carried the briefcase up to the living room, laid it across her coffee table, and slid open the latch.

Three yellow legal pads, filled out in Delroy's loopy, semi-illegible handwriting, tumbled onto the coffee table. Long after everyone else had abandoned writing things out by hand in favor of Microsoft Word, Delroy had insisted on doing things the old-fashioned way. Looking at the legal pads, Bertie was overcome by a wave of longing so visceral she could taste it. The paper even smelled like Delroy. Steeling herself, she took a seat on the couch, picked up the legal pad closest to her, and began to read:

THE CHICAGOAN—A LAWYER'S JOURNEY
BY DELROY ANTHONY BIGELOW

When I moved to Chicago in 1993, I never imagined
I'd spend the rest of my life here. I was born and raised

*in Harlem and had just graduated from NYU. I was a
cocky city kid and didn't think there was anything that
could keep me away from the Big Apple longer than
the three years it would take me to finish law school at
the University of Chicago. Even after I established a
successful practice on the city's vibrant South Side, I'd
always planned to return to Harlem someday. But all
that changed the day I met Bertie Henderson.*

Pausing only to wipe away her tears, Bertie read steadily for the
next hour. It was just like Delroy to keep his book a secret. Most likely,
he'd been planning to present it to her on their wedding anniversary.
He'd written about everything—their courtship and marriage, his
first job working for a large law firm in the Loop, and his decision to
leave that firm to go into private practice.

As she began to read the next yellow legal pad, Bertie understood
why Delroy had asked Judge Green to review his manuscript. In *Book
Two—Significant Cases*, Delroy discussed his biggest legal victories
in vivid detail. The discrimination suit he won against a well-known
hotel chain that somehow never managed to make rooms available
for African American travelers. The libel suit he'd won after a local
talk radio host repeatedly characterized Dr. Momolu Taylor as an
"ignorant voodoo witchdoctor." The wrongful death suit against
Delvaine PharmaCorp that netted an impoverished South Side family
nearly five million dollars. Now that the cases had been settled, Delroy
pulled no punches. He named names and offered candid accounts of
his many courtroom battles.

On the last legal pad, Delroy had started work on a new section
called *Book Three—Making a Difference*. Unlike the polished prose
of the first two sections, *Book Three* consisted largely of sentence
fragments. As she skimmed over the pages, Bertie smiled and blew
her nose for what seemed like the millionth time that night. How
many times had she teased Delroy about his obsession with collecting

things? African masks, Civil War memorabilia, first editions by black authors—anything connected with African American history drew Delroy like a moth to the flame. From what Bertie could surmise, *Book Three* had been Delroy's people collection. Although clearly unfinished, it contained thumbnail biographies of community leaders: Alderman Fred Clark; Silas Blackstone, the founder of Chicago's largest African American bank; Charley Howard, the Hot Sauce King; Dr. Momolu Taylor at the Princeton Avenue Natural Health Clinic; and Karen Phillips, the "teacher's teacher" who, frustrated with the poor quality of Chicago's public school system, started an afterschool program that now serves more than a thousand teenagers.

Under each person's name, Delroy had compiled a list of facts. When and where born, colleges attended, marriages, awards, and honorary degrees. With a smile, Bertie noted that her husband had already managed to amass a few surprising biographical tidbits. While at college, "Steady Freddy" Clark had nearly been expelled for cheating on a history test. Karen Phillips was ten years older than she let on, according to the date of birth Delroy had placed beside her name. His notes also revealed that the dynamic school reformer had been married twice before moving to the South Side in 1990. Dr. Momolu Taylor claimed to be related to Togar Henries, the Liberian diamond magnate. According to Delroy's notes, the Henries family had never heard of him. Next to the doctor's entry, Delroy had made a note to *Check with USICS* in red ink.

Though Bertie knew that Charley Howard had had a rough life before becoming the Hot Sauce King, she had no idea he had been arrested for assault and battery. According to Delroy's notes, Howard was suspected of beating up the chairman of his condo association, a Mr. Elmer Jones. The case had been dropped when Mr. Jones decided not to press charges. Nor had she been aware that the cautious banker Silas Blackstone had sired an illegitimate child during the flamboyantly bohemian summer he'd spent in Morocco after his first year in business school. Once again, Delroy had added a note to himself next to Blackstone's entry—*Child still living? Regrets?*

On the very last page, Theophilous Green had written his critique in a crisp, precise hand. *Re: Actionable nature of MS: Verify all docs— birth certs., crim. hist., citizenshp papers, etc. Re-depose before pub.— audi alteram partem!*

Audi alteram partem. Although she'd picked up a smattering of Latin phrases from Delroy over the years, Bertie had never heard this one before. Trust Theophilous to come up with something obscure, she thought to herself. Poor old fool. Wonder what it means? If anyone would know arcane legal terminology, it was her late husband's colleague David Mackenzie.

She picked up her cell phone and punched in the lawyer's number.

When he answered, Mac's voice, although friendly enough, lacked its customary enthusiasm.

"I just had a quick question," Bertie said. "If this is a bad time, I can call back later."

"Nonsense," Mackenzie said. "What can I do for you?"

"I was just wondering if you know what *audi alteram partem* means. Is it a legal term?"

"What on earth makes you want to know about that?"

"It would take too long to explain over the phone," Bertie said. "Please. Can you tell me what it means?"

"Literally it means 'to hear from the other side.' It reminds the judge to hear from both parties before making a final decision. What's going on here, Bertie?" Mackenzie teased. "Don't tell me you've decided to study for the bar."

"Oh, no, nothing like that," Bertie said hastily. "I'll tell you all about it some other time."

"What about Friday?" Mackenzie suggested. "Come to the house for dinner. I'm curious what's got you speaking Latin all of a sudden."

"I don't want to impose. I'm probably interrupting you as it is."

"Don't be ridiculous," Mackenzie said. "Angie and I would love to see you. I'll ask her to make us all some gumbo."

"As long as it's not too much trouble," Bertie said. "I'll fill you in on the rest of the story when I see you."

As Bertie hung up the phone, she felt a shiver move up her spine. Theophilous had been telling Delroy to "hear from the other side." What on earth had he meant by this remark? Did it even matter anymore? Nine months ago, Delroy Bigelow and Theophilous had been making big plans for the future. Now, all that remained of their hopes and dreams were a few pages of cryptic notes. Both men were dead, and one of them had been murdered.

Chapter Seven

Ten days after the murder, Judge Green's funeral was held with due pomp and circumstance at Trinity Episcopal Church. Built in 1893, the stately gothic cathedral on the edge of Chicago's Historic Bronzeville District had been ministering to upwardly mobile black folks for over sixty years. As Bertie, Ellen, and a well-dressed collection of Chicago's African American elite looked on, Mayor Davis gave a moving tribute, dusting off his Latin to end with a quote from the Roman historian, Pliny.

"Judge Theophilus Green left this world full of years and full of honors. *Plennus annis ablit, plenus honoribus.*"

After the Mayor's speech, the Reverend Bryant J. McCall launched into what promised to be a lengthy eulogy. In the second pew, Alderman Fred Clark, his lanky frame draped in a black suit hand-tailored from raw silk, crossed one leg over the other and stole a glance at his Rolex. His black, cashmere overcoat hung casually over the back of the pew in front of him. *That coat must have set him back at least five hundred dollars,* Bertie thought to herself. It would certainly qualify in anyone's book as a "fancy coat." Was Alderman Clark the angry man who had waited for LaShawn Thomas at Mrs. Petty's house? If so, why?

The more Bertie thought about her wayward student, the more conflicted she became. She still had no idea what had possessed the boy to attack the alderman at the Christmas concert. Nor did she have a clue what LaShawn had been doing at Jackson Towers the night of Judge Green's murder. Had she done the right thing in not telling Detective Kulicki she'd seen him there?

Dr. Momolu Taylor sat two rows back, his arm draped casually over Patrice Soule's shoulder. Regally attired in a long African robe embroidered with gold, the doctor's expression ranged between boredom and irritation as the minister droned on. From what Bertie could tell, Taylor and the judge had not been the best of friends. Could the fact that Judge Green was head over heels in lust with Patrice Soule have had anything to do with their enmity?

Charley Howard, the Hot Sauce King, sat with his wife on the other side of the church. Next to Howard's massive bulk, Mabel Howard seemed insubstantial, almost wraithlike. As the minister continued to speak, Bertie peeked surreptitiously at Howard's face. Was Howard glad the judge was dead? With Theophilous out of the way, his application for membership in the Octagon Society was sure to be accepted. With the notable exception of Mrs. Leflore, the Society's membership committee was made up of younger, less conservative types who'd be eager to welcome the Hot Sauce King—and his money—into the fold. According to Delroy's manuscript, Howard had been arrested for assault and battery, although his victim had refused to press charges. Could Howard have been angry enough with the judge to kill him?

The sound of shuffling feet as the congregation stood for the final hymn snapped Bertie from her reverie. *Stop this idle speculation this instant,* she said to herself. For all she knew, the police were closing in on Judge Green's killer this very minute.

At precisely seven fifteen the following evening, Bertie walked up the three cement stairs that led to David Mackenzie's townhouse. The Mackenzies lived in South Commons, a warren of townhouses located minutes from the heart of the Loop. It had been snowing all afternoon, and with all the traffic on Lake Shore Drive, Bertie had been afraid she would be late. Other than her disastrous evening with Theophilous Green, it was the first time Bertie had been out to a social occasion in months. In one hand, she carried a bottle of French Bordeaux and in the other, a foil-wrapped plate of homemade brownies. Hopefully, if the Mackenzies didn't like French wine they would at least enjoy the brownies. She took a deep breath and rang the buzzer.

Seconds later, the door flew open and Big Mac, dressed for comfort in a University of Illinois sweatshirt and a pair of well-worn jeans, enveloped her in a bear hug.

"Welcome, stranger," he boomed. "Come in out of the cold."

"I'll be out in a minute to say hello," Angelique called out from the kitchen. "Mac's got me sweating over a hot stove back here."

"I brought you guys wine and chocolate," Bertie said. "Need any help?"

Angelique laughed. "Nah. I've been making gumbo since I was ten. I'm sipping on some Wild Turkey and catching up on old *Scandal* reruns. I'll be out in a bit. Just make yourself at home."

The house smelled of onions, peppers, and tomatoes simmering in olive oil. Miles Davis's trumpet shimmered softly from the Bose speakers recessed into the ceiling, and signed prints by Jacob Lawrence, Romare Bearden, and Elizabeth Catlett lined the walls. A small gas fireplace burning in the corner gave their dining room a cozy elegance.

As she and Mac exchanged pleasantries, Bertie recalled the many times she and Delroy had visited here. It sure felt different being there alone. Resolutely, she pushed aside the grief that threatened to overwhelm her. Much as she missed Delroy, she had to get out and socialize. Otherwise, she was likely to turn into one of those people one saw on reality TV—the hermits who stayed indoors for years at a time and hoarded things.

Angelique's gumbo was delicious—mild, but with just enough red pepper to highlight the tomato, okra, and shrimp that gave the dish its flavor. As they ate, Bertie and the Mackenzies worked their way through two bottles of crisp German Riesling as they discussed old times and mutual friends—people Bertie and Delroy had socialized with before her husband's sudden death. No one brought up Judge Theophilous Green's murder until after the dinner dishes had been cleared away nearly two hours later.

"You must have been one of the last people to see Theophilous alive," Angelique said, giving Bertie a speculative glance. "I didn't know the two of you were so close."

"We weren't close," Bertie said. Perhaps because she did not wish to speak ill of the dead, or more likely because she just didn't feel like reliving the incident, she omitted the harrowing details of her visit to Judge Green's apartment. "I couldn't go to the Octagon Ball without a date. I wanted to hear the Count Basie Orchestra, and Theophilous offered to be my escort. It was that simple."

"Nothing simple about it," Angelique said. "The man is dead." Carefully, she lifted the antique decanter from the sideboard next to the table and splashed a healthy dose of bourbon into her glass. "Don't suppose you shot him, did you?"

"No," Bertie said calmly. "Sorry to disappoint you." Mackenzie's wife was apparently trying to rattle her, but Bertie was determined to maintain her dignity. With a chilly smile, she changed the subject. "When I went to the judge's apartment that night, I learned my husband had been working on a memoir. He'd left it with Judge Green for safekeeping. You could have knocked me over with a feather when Theophilous showed it to me. I didn't know a thing about it."

"Delroy definitely had a secretive side," Mac said. "What was he writing about?"

"Some of it is about the cases he won—who did what to whom and when. Some of it is his life story. And some of it is about the movers and shakers he knew on the South Side."

"I've been President of the Jack and Jill Charity Fund Drive for the past three years," Angelique said. "Am I in it?"

Bertie shook her head.

"Well, what about David then?" Angelique tossed off the remaining bourbon in her glass and poured herself another. "A former Cook County prosecutor, now in private practice. That should count for something, right?"

While Bertie cast about in her mind for a tactful response, Big Mac shook his head in irritation.

"Who cares, Angie? That's not even the point."

"I care, that's who!" Mackenzie's wife shouted. By this point in the evening, she'd consumed a fair amount of liquor. But far from being a mellowing influence, the alcohol seemed to make Angelique even more irritable. "That's just like you, Mac. You don't stick up for yourself. You're so oblivious you don't even know when you're being dissed."

"I'm sure Delroy meant no disrespect," Bertie said mildly. "There are only a few people in this section. Politicians and entrepreneurs, mostly. Alderman Clark, Silas Blackstone, the president of Unity Bank, Charley Howard. People like that."

"Charley Howard? The Hot Sauce King?" Angelique sniffed derisively. "That man's nothing but a cheap hoodlum. Everybody knows he's a front man for the Roselli mob."

"Maybe he is, and maybe he isn't," Mac said. "You shouldn't say things like that about people you don't know."

Angelique ignored him. "Did you say Freddy Clark was in the manuscript, Bertie?"

Bertie nodded reluctantly. As the hostility level in the room rose, she realized that Mac and his wife probably argued like this on a regular basis. The last thing she wanted to do was to add fuel to the fire.

"Like I said, the manuscript was unfinished. More like a rough sketch, really. Perhaps if Delroy had lived, he would have added more chapters," Bertie said in what she hoped was a placating tone.

"Give me a break," Angelique snapped. "Steady Freddy's got to be as crooked as a dog's hind leg."

"How do you know he's crooked?" Big Mac said. "You've never even met the man."

"Come off it, David. How the hell else did he get elected? Those politicians are all the same, especially on the South Side. I'll bet you Freddy's taking bribes from every gangbanger in Englewood. If you took your nose out of those stupid law books once in a while, you'd know that."

Although the lawyer was trying to keep his cool, Bertie could see that his wife's needling was beginning to get to him.

"You can't just go around saying things like that about people," Mac said. "You don't have a scintilla of evidence to support that statement."

"David Mackenzie, legal eagle," Angelique said. As she waved her glass in the air, her voice dripped with sarcasm. "The patron saint of losers the world over."

"I'm warning you," Mackenzie said. "Give it a rest. Now."

"Or what?" Angelique fixed her husband with a challenging glare. "What exactly do you plan to do about it, David? Tell me!"

"Please, Angie," Mackenzie said softly. "Now is not the time or place."

"It's never the time or place for you," Angelique said bitterly. "We haven't had a real conversation in ten years." Wobbling unsteadily, she pushed back from the table and stood up. "Sorry to break up this little gathering, but I'm feeling a bit under the weather."

"I ought to go," Bertie said. "Let you get some rest."

"No need to rush off," Angelique said. Mac looked daggers in her direction as she staggered to the sideboard and poured herself another shot of bourbon. "We both know you've been waiting all night to get my husband alone."

David Mackenzie slammed his fist onto the table. "That's enough!" he shouted. "I will not have you behaving like this in front of our guest."

"Bastard!" Angelique hissed. As Bertie stared, open-mouthed, Angelique Mackenzie drained the rest of the brandy in her glass and stumbled out of the room.

In the pause that followed, Mac shook his head like a fighter who'd just absorbed a hard right to the head.

"Jesus, Bertie. I don't know what gets into Angie sometimes," he said slowly. "She didn't mean it, really she didn't. It's just the liquor talking."

Bertie wasn't too sure about that. But now was certainly not the time to discuss it.

"Don't worry about it," she said, giving Mackenzie a sympathetic pat on the shoulder. "Go take care of your wife. I can see myself out."

Lake Shore Drive was virtually deserted on the way home. As she made her way along the dark and snowy streets, Bertie couldn't help but ask herself why it was that a good man like David Mackenzie was burdened with a drunken shrew like Angelique. If Delroy were alive, she would have asked him. Perhaps another man would be able to understand such a thing. It sure seemed a shame, though, she thought to herself. Mac is far too good for Angelique. Always was and always would be.

Chapter Eight

FRIDAY, JANUARY 18, 2013—7:00 A.M.

One week later, Detective Michael Kulicki rang Bertie's doorbell at seven in the morning. As seemed to be his custom, the detective was unshaven and looked like he hadn't slept in a week. As Bertie opened her front door, he took one last drag on a cigarette before flicking the butt into the street.

"Your Smith & Wesson has checked out clean," he said, handing Bertie the shoebox that contained her gun.

Though she wanted to keep her demeanor crisp and professional, Bertie couldn't resist a smile.

"Does this mean I'm no longer a suspect?"

Kulicki's eyes narrowed, and he studied Bertie for a full beat before answering.

"This is an ongoing investigation, Mrs. Bigelow. We are continuing to look into everyone who was with the judge the night he died. Do not leave the city without letting me know."

As the detective drove away, Bertie felt a chill work its way up her spine. Surely the cops didn't really think she was a murderer? She'd read somewhere that ten thousand people in the US were wrongly convicted of crimes every year. Was she about to become one of them? It would have been nice if Kulicki could have offered some kind of reassurance, let her know she was not going to be dragged out of her house in handcuffs. Instead, he'd told her not to leave town.

As she climbed up the stairs to the kitchen and put a kettle of water on for tea, Bertie tried her best to push these unpleasant thoughts from her mind. It didn't help her mood that LaShawn Thomas was not returning her calls and had apparently gone into hiding. Worse still, she could only assume that her longstanding friendship with David and Angelique Mackenzie was now on shaky ground. It was never advisable to get in the middle of a fight between two married people. Now that she had witnessed the seamy underbelly of their relationship, Angie and Mac might very well close ranks and banish her from their lives entirely. Mackenzie had always been a valued friend, the only man she felt she could confide in. How she would manage if he were to disappear from her life was something Bertie did not want to contemplate.

All in all, the past three weeks had been a continuous nightmare. Christmas vacation had come and gone in a blur of nonstop stress, and now Metro College was back in session. Sadly, it was not possible to hop the next plane to a remote and preferably uninhabited tropical island. But at the very least she could put her worries aside for the rest of the day.

After devouring a sinfully delicious breakfast of hash browns, sausage, and scrambled eggs, Bertie took a long bubble bath, steaming up the bathroom mirrors and topping off the tub until the hot water ran out. One hour later, dressed in a warm down coat, work boots, a Metro College sweatshirt, and her favorite pair of jeans, Bertie got in her car and drove to the Near North Side.

Along Southport Avenue, an assortment of Chicago's rising young professionals, apparently oblivious to the brisk winter wind blowing in from Lake Michigan, strolled, jogged, walked their dogs, and browsed in trendy little shops. It was still early in the day, and Bertie was able to snag a parking spot on the street. Her destination, an old movie theater that had been lovingly restored to its original Baroque splendor, was just around the corner. Once inside, she took off her coat, set her cell phone to vibrate, and settled comfortably in her seat.

For the rest of the afternoon nothing would be allowed to distract her from the spectacle of Humphrey Bogart and Lauren Bacall flickering larger than life across the silver screen.

It was almost dark when Bertie emerged from the theater. Tiny snow crystals glistened in the glow of the street lamps on Waveland Avenue and crunched under her feet on the sidewalk. Her cell phone, still set to vibrate, buzzed like an angry bee in her pocket. Bertie ignored the call. As she brushed the snow off her windshield, the phone buzzed again. Again, she ignored it. When the device went off two minutes later, Bertie heaved a sigh, extracted it from her pocket, and peered at the caller ID. When she saw her boss's Metro College extension flash across the screen, Bertie's heart rate quickened.

"I was beginning to think you'd been arrested," Dr. Grant's executive assistant said in her well-modulated voice. A gray-haired dynamo in her mid-forties, Hedda Eberhardt was the power behind the throne at Metro College. Among the faculty, she was referred to as the Dragon of Doom. "The chancellor wants to see you the minute he comes back from his vacation."

"Do you have any idea why?" Bertie's words tumbled out in a rush of anxiety. "Is it about the concert?"

"You know I'm not at liberty to discuss that," Eberhardt said crisply. "The college will be closed Monday for the Martin Luther King holiday. Be in his office Tuesday morning at nine sharp. Don't be late."

For the rest of the weekend, Bertie worried about her upcoming meeting with Chancellor Grant. Recalling the near-apoplectic expression on his face on the night of the concert, it was easy to surmise that the meeting would not be pleasant. The only real question was the degree of unpleasantness she would have to endure. Although she tried her best to stay cheerful, visions of the chancellor, looking a lot like Ebeneezer Scrooge in *A Christmas Carol*, haunted her dreams.

Fortunately, Monday was Martin Luther King Day—a day to put aside the mundane and focus on the big picture. If it wasn't for

Martin and the thousands of anonymous Civil Rights warriors who had sacrificed their lives for equal rights, Bertie was well aware she would never have been hired to teach at a college. Instead, she'd have been relegated to the same kind of jobs her grandmother had to perform—cleaning homes and washing white folks' dirty clothes. Bertie celebrated King Day every year by attending a black history breakfast at St. Mark Methodist Church. Despite the tragic events of the past three weeks, she was determined to maintain the tradition.

Chapter Nine

Rubbing the sleep from her eyes, Bertie Bigelow rolled out of bed, splashed some cold water on her face, and staggered into the kitchen. As she stood groggily, waiting for the kettle to boil, the phone rang.

"Mrs. B?" The voice on the other end of the line was soft and hesitant.

"Speak up. I can barely hear you," she said. "Who is this?"

"It's LaShawn Thomas." In a louder and somewhat injured tone, the young man continued. "You know. From school."

The kid should have begun this call with an apology, Bertie thought sourly.

"I don't have time to fool with you now, LaShawn. I drove all the way out to your house to see you. You should have talked to me then."

"I'm sorry, Mrs. B. Do you hate me?"

"Of course not," Bertie said quickly. "But I can't say I'm happy. What on earth is going on? It must be important, or you wouldn't be calling me so early in the morning."

"Damn right, it's important." LaShawn's voice rose an octave. "I'm in *jail*. The police say I killed Judge Green. But it's a lie, Mrs. B. I thought since your husband was a big-time lawyer and all, maybe you could help me."

For the past eighteen months, Bertie had nurtured this boy, helping him transform himself from sullen outcast into Dean's List material.

54

True, he'd disappointed her. But murder? It was just not possible. Or was it?

"Be honest with me," she said. "I know you were at the Jackson Towers that night. I saw you go inside."

"Of course I was there," LaShawn said impatiently. "I was working. The Princeton Avenue Natural Health Clinic asked me to take a package over there, which I did. But that's *all* I did. I sure didn't kill nobody. I never shot a gun in my whole life!"

"There's got to be some mistake. Where are they holding you?"

"I'm at the District Three lockup," he said. "Grand Crossing. You know it?"

Bertie's stomach tightened. Of course she knew it. Last year two prisoners there had died from "unknown causes."

"I'm no lawyer, but I'll see what I can do. I'm on my way. Sit tight, and don't say a word to anyone until I get there."

Bertie punched Big Mac's home number into her cell phone. They had not spoken since Angelique's drunken meltdown on Friday night. It was entirely possible Mac would feel uncomfortable talking to her. However, this was a matter of life and death. If anyone was capable of getting her student out of that infamous holding facility, it was Mac.

"I hate to bother you, but I don't know where else to turn," she told him. He listened quietly as she explained the situation.

"Don't worry," he said. "I'll meet you at the police station in half an hour."

Although the Grand Crossing lockup was only three miles from Bertie's home, it might as well have been on another planet. The bustling neighborhood of stores, apartment buildings, and churches she remembered from her childhood days had become a vast urban desert. Block after block stood empty—no people, no businesses, no homes. On the side streets where the black middle-class folks of her parents' generation had proudly staked their claim on the American Dream, gang violence ran rampant. The Conquering Lions, the Gangster Disciples, and the Vice Lords waged war on a nightly basis for control of these streets. In the past six months alone, nearly one hundred shootings had taken place in the two-square-mile area between 70th and 80th Streets and Cottage Grove and King Drive.

By the time she pulled into the parking lot behind the bleak, windowless, white bunker that housed the District Three Police Station, Bertie Bigelow was in a foul mood. Big Mac was waiting for her in the lobby.

"Wait here, Bertie," he said. "I'll talk to the cops and find out what's going on." After a brief conversation with the officer on duty, he was buzzed through a metal checkpoint and disappeared.

Bertie took a seat in one of the black, plastic chairs positioned against the wall. As she waited for Mackenzie's return, she watched a weary parade of humanity stream in and out of the police station. Victims lined up at the front desk to report crimes—houses broken into, cars stolen, dreams destroyed. In a separate line, friends, relatives, and lawyers of prisoners waited patiently to have their IDs checked by the beleaguered officer on duty.

When Mac returned a few minutes later, his face was grim.

"Did you get to see LaShawn?" she asked, struggling to keep up with the burly lawyer's pace as they strode outside into the frigid January day.

"Oh, I've seen him alright." Mackenzie turned to face her. "We need to talk. Can you follow me back to Hyde Park? Maybe we can get some breakfast. This place depresses me."

Once they'd settled into a corner booth at Salonica Diner, a cozy, low-budget hangout near the University of Chicago, Mackenzie spoke.

"Look Bertie, about what happened Friday night. I just want to say how sorry I am."

"No need to apologize," Bertie said. "These things happen. Is Angelique alright?"

Mac shrugged. "I suppose. She's been flying off the handle like that a lot lately. Drinking too much. Making scenes."

"Have you talked to her, Mac?"

"I've tried," Mac said. "Of course I've tried. She says I work too much. Says I don't pay attention to her, treat her like furniture."

Bertie sighed. "Have you thought about going to see a marriage counselor?"

Big Mac reached across the table and patted Bertie gently on the arm.

"Don't try to solve my problems for me, okay? This is something I've got to handle on my own."

Bertie blushed and looked down. "The last thing I'd want to do is get in your business."

After an awkward pause, the lawyer cleared his throat.

"Well. On to Mr. LaShawn Thomas then." He blew on his coffee, then took a sip. "I'm not so sure it's a good idea for you to get mixed up in this thing, Bertie. After all, the judge was a friend of yours."

Bertie grimaced. "I don't know if friend is really the right word. LaShawn is my student, David. I know him. He's bright, and he's talented. I just can't believe he'd do anything like this. What did he tell you?"

"He does admit knowing Judge Green. And get this—he says it's not the first time he's dropped by the judge's apartment late at night. The way he tells it, he and the judge were friends."

"Really?"

"That's what he says. I would more likely use the term acquaintances, but, in any case, it seems he and Green had some connection." Big Mac leaned forward. "And this is where it gets really crazy. LaShawn says he's been supplying the old man with weekly doses of a male hormone supplement called Testemaxx."

"Testemaxx?" Bertie raised an eyebrow. *No wonder Theophilous was such a horny old bastard.*

"Yeah," Mac said, blushing slightly. "LaShawn says the stuff comes in an inhaler. It's stronger than Viagra, plus it takes effect immediately."

"How in the world would LaShawn get hold of something like that?"

"He says he was delivering the stuff for the Princeton Avenue Natural Health Clinic," Mac said.

"When Dr. Taylor opened that clinic three years ago, my husband helped him get his paperwork together," Bertie said. "As I remember, there was some controversy involved."

Big Mac laughed. "That's putting it mildly. It was an all-out war. The *Chicago Tribune* called Taylor an 'ignorant witchdoctor,' and the county sheriff tried to shut him down. Your late husband had to file an antidiscrimination suit just to get the clinic licensed."

"Having been through such an ordeal, it's hard to imagine Dr. Taylor would want to be associated with anything even remotely out of the ordinary."

"That's exactly what I thought," Mac said. "How stable is this kid? I heard about what he did at the Christmas concert. Is there any chance LaShawn could be making this up?"

"It's hard to say, given his behavior. Obviously, he's got a serious grudge against Alderman Clark. But he's not a killer, Mac. He's just not the type."

"You'd be surprised," Mac said. "No offense, but you can be a bit of a Pollyanna when it comes to assessing people."

"Guilty as charged, Counselor," Bertie said. "I suppose I would look even more foolish if I told you I knew LaShawn was at the Jackson Towers New Year's Eve but didn't tell the cops about it."

Mac put down his fork and gave Bertie a stern look.

"You would look very foolish, indeed. Don't tell me you've been withholding evidence."

"I didn't exactly *withhold* evidence," Bertie said carefully. "I just didn't volunteer anything. That's different."

"What in the world's gotten into you, Bertie? What makes you so sure this boy is innocent?"

"As a teacher, you get a gut feeling about kids," Bertie said. "A certain look in their eye when they've cheated on a test. The way they stand when they really want to sing the solo but are too shy to step forward. Call it women's intuition, if you like. But I know LaShawn would never kill anyone." Bertie buttered her blueberry pancakes and covered them with a generous river of maple syrup. She knew she'd have to pay for this indulgence at the gym later on, but this morning seemed to call for unusual measures. "So many of my students walk in the door with the deck stacked against them. I know it sounds corny, but I believe they deserve a chance. Truth is, I'm an inveterate optimist."

"And I am an ex-prosecutor. We're talking about Theophilus A. Green, the first African American ever to join the Illinois Supreme Court. It seems unlikely LaShawn even knew this guy."

"Then why was he in the judge's apartment? Are you telling me that out of all the apartments in Jackson Towers, LaShawn just happened to pick Theophilous's place?"

"The judge was an elderly man who lived alone. He would have been an easy target. According to the police report, the apartment had been ransacked. The judge's credit cards, laptop, and cell phone are missing. Worst of all, the police found the murder weapon in a dumpster behind Jackson Towers. The kid's prints are on it. They're smudged, and they're not the only prints, but they're there."

"LaShawn could be telling the truth about those testosterone supplements. I'd hoped I wouldn't have to talk about this, but maybe I should." Steadying herself with a deep breath, Bertie gave the lawyer a blow-by-blow account of her visit to the judge's apartment.

"Good thing I didn't know about this," Mac said. "I'd have gone over there and shot the old bastard myself. You alright?"

"I'm dealing with it."

"It tears me up to think about someone treating you that way." Impulsively, Mac reached across the table and squeezed Bertie's hand. "If there's anything I can do to help—anything at all—just ask."

Bertie nodded. As Mac's hand continued to rest gently over her own, Bertie became intensely aware of its warm and comforting presence. How long had it been since a man had touched her like that? *Steady, girl*, Bertie told herself. Taking a deep breath, she withdrew her hand and placed it carefully in her lap.

"Both you and Angelique have already done so much for me," she said. "Please tell her how much I appreciate her letting let me drag you down here. I wouldn't have done it if they'd put LaShawn in a different holding facility. But prisoners have died in the Grand Crossing lockup, Mac."

"It's okay. Angie was already on her way out when you called. Said she was going to meet some friends for brunch." Turning his face away from Bertie, Mac stopped talking and stared bleakly through the plate-glass window at the cars passing on 57th Street.

After a moment, the burly lawyer cleared his throat.

"Look here. Normally, no one cares what happens to the guys in the lockup, but Detective Kulicki owes me a ton of favors. I'll ask him to keep an eye on LaShawn tonight."

"Then what?"

"He'll have a bond hearing sometime tomorrow. If I can convince the judge that LaShawn is not likely to leave the state, he'll be allowed out on bond until his trial. But don't mount up that white horse just yet." Mackenzie leaned forward and looked Bertie in the eye. "I've had a lot of experience with these kinds of cases. Your student is lying to you. It is entirely possible LaShawn Thomas is nothing but a cold-blooded murderer."

Chapter Ten

TUESDAY, JANUARY 22, 2013—6:30 A.M.

When Bertie woke up and looked out her window the next morning, she groaned out loud. Eight inches of snow had fallen during the night. As she contemplated the day ahead, she suppressed the urge to pull the covers up over her head and hide. Snow or no snow, she absolutely had to get to work on time. The last thing in the world she needed was to be late for her nine o'clock appointment with Chancellor Grant.

The fact that he was having her come in on his first day back from Christmas vacation struck her as ominous, to say the least. If Delroy were here, he would have taken her in his arms and told her not to worry. While the two of them shared a cozy breakfast, he'd have reminded her how difficult it is to fire a faculty member with tenure. Then he'd have gone outside and shoveled off the sidewalk, spread a protective layer of salt crystals on the front steps, and excavated both their cars. If Delroy were here . . . But he wasn't. Rapid and lethal as an avalanche, memories of her dead husband engulfed her. Tears stung her eyes and splashed down her cheeks onto the bedspread. If only Delroy were here . . .

Whoa, girl. Keep it together. This is no time for a meltdown. Willing herself out of bed, Bertie tugged on her winter coat, pulled a pair of no-nonsense galoshes over her shoes, grabbed her snow shovel, and stepped out into the bright winter morning.

"Top o' the mornin' to ya," Colleen O'Fallon shouted, cheerfully flinging shovelfuls of snow into a large pile alongside the curb. Colleen and her twin sister, Pat, were retired schoolteachers who had moved to Chicago from Ireland in the 1970s. As far as Bertie could tell, the two women had lived in the house next door ever since. Both sisters were thin with translucent skin, halos of white hair, and watery blue eyes that did not miss a trick.

"Who's that, Collie?" Pat O'Fallon, dressed in a vintage, beige overcoat with a matching scarf and green wool cap, peeked out from behind the tail fins of their 1978 Oldsmobile, snow shovel in hand. "Is that Bertie?"

"The very same, Pat. Who else would ya be expectin'?"

Ignoring her sister, Pat said, "Grand little snowfall we're havin', eh, Bertie?"

"Lovely," Bertie agreed with an ironic smile. From the moment she and Delroy had moved into the neighborhood, the O'Fallon sisters, who had no children of their own, had watched their comings and goings with the same lively interest with which other people watched the soaps on daytime TV.

"We were thinking ya'd never make it out here," Pat continued, chopping vigorously at a stubborn patch of ice. "After all, you've probably got other things on your mind."

"Sure she does," Colleen added. "What with the police stoppin' by and all."

"*Especially* with the police stoppin' by," Pat said. "Not to mention all the other visitors comin' and goin' at all hours. Quite naturally. You've been havin' developments. Isn't that right, Bertie?"

With the focused intention of two hungry sparrows, the O'Fallon sisters cocked their heads inquiringly. Bertie sighed. While she cleared what felt like a ton of snow from the top of her car to a pile alongside the curb, Bertie told the two women about Judge Green's death and Detective Kulicki's subsequent visits.

"I *told* you Bertie knew that judge, now didn't I, Pat?" Colleen stuck a shovel triumphantly atop the snow pile she'd created and poked her sister in the ribs.

"You did no such thing," Pat retorted. "That's just your style, now isn't it? Always tryin' to grab the glory. I was the one who saw his picture in the paper, not you. 'Twas me that said the man looked like Bertie's type. *I* was the one."

Inwardly, Bertie groaned. She did not have the time or inclination to ask the two white women exactly what they meant about the judge being her "type." Presumably, it meant that, like Bertie, he was a light-skinned African American. When it came to matters of race these days, nothing was ever as simple as it seemed. Pleased to have avoided at least one misstep on the mine-strewn battlefield of race relations, Bertie retired indoors and got dressed for work.

She walked into the sprawling Metro College complex two hours later. Thanks to an influx of federal funds in the 1990s, the college had a shiny glass building that contained the auditorium, a state-of-the-art computer lab, and the administrative offices. Most of the actual teaching, however, went on in the same ramshackle structure that had housed the school since the 1950s. After checking her email messages, Bertie dropped into the faculty lounge for a cup of coffee. The dingy, windowless room was packed with teachers and buzzing with gossip.

"I'm assuming you've all read about our Golden Boy," Maria Francione said. A forty-something redhead known for her quick wit and fiery temper, Francione was the school's drama teacher. "Listen to this," she said, picking up a copy of the paper and adjusting her reading glasses. *"LaShawn Thomas, a twenty-year-old student at Metro Community College, has been arrested in connection with the murder of Judge Theophilus Green. Although he continues to maintain his innocence, Thomas has admitted that he was in the judge's apartment on the night of the murder. 'Judge Green was my friend,' Thomas stated."*

Jack Ivers, who had taught political science at Metro College since 1983, waved a dismissive hand.

"Give me a break. What judge in his right mind would be friends with a kid like that?"

With his rumpled suit and shaggy gray hair, Jack Ivers was idolized by many of the younger faculty for his outspoken opposition to Big Government. Ellen Simpson couldn't stand him. Colorful as always in an orange-and-black dress from Ghana, she rolled her eyes at Bertie before wading into the conversation.

"And why couldn't LaShawn be telling the truth," Ellen said. "What makes you such an expert on the boy's behavior, Jack?"

Jack Ivers fixed her with a baleful stare. "It doesn't take an expert to see the kid's a natural-born con man. I'll grant you he's intelligent, but I wouldn't trust him as far as I could throw him."

"LaShawn is way too bright to commit such a stupid crime," Maria Francione snapped. "He might talk someone to death, but he wouldn't shoot him. What do you think, Bertie? You're the one whose concert he ruined."

All eyes swiveled to Bertie, who'd been doing her best to stay out of the argument.

"I have no idea why he wrecked the Christmas concert," she said slowly. "All I know is LaShawn had tears in his eyes when he was finished."

"Real tears?" Maria Francione clapped her hands in mock applause. "What did I tell you? A first-rate dramatic talent."

Letitia Petrowski, the stout bottle blonde who taught chemistry, could hardly contain her irritation.

"Sure, the boy is bright. Sure, he's talented. But look what he comes from. His whole family's either dead, on welfare, or in jail. Something was bound to go wrong sooner or later."

"That is exactly the problem," Ellen said, shaking her head in disgust. "Teachers like you expect nothing, therefore, he thinks of himself as nothing and acts accordingly."

"I went out of my way to help that boy," Petrowski said, her pale cheeks red with anger. "You people are all alike. Maybe it's not 'PC' to say it, but our students have problems. Serious problems."

Among the faculty at Metro College, political debate had become something of a blood sport. If Petrowski, who'd been at Metro less than a year, had been to more of these bull sessions, she would probably have chosen her words more carefully.

"Teachers like you have failed this community time and time again," Ellen said, wagging her finger in Petrowski's face. "Did you ever stop to think why our students are having problems?"

"I don't have to stop and think why," Letitia fired back. "It's because these people are beyond dysfunctional. Drug dealers. Gangbangers. Illiterate welfare queens with no ambition in life other than making babies and smoking crack."

Ellen's eyes narrowed, and she leaned back, rocking slightly like a cobra getting ready to strike. *Letitia doesn't know it yet, but she's about to be road kill,* Bertie thought to herself.

"Did you just use the term 'illiterate welfare queen'? I have a strong suspicion our chancellor might consider your remarks to be racist. Certainly, they do not befit a person who has been entrusted with educating our city's disadvantaged children." Ellen stepped closer to the science teacher, her bracelets clanking menacingly as she delivered her *coup de grâce.* "Do you have tenure, Miss Petrowski?"

Dumbfounded at the vitriol that had just flown out of Ellen's mouth, the science teacher said nothing.

Ellen gave a satisfied grunt. "No tenure? I thought so. Perhaps I should send Dr. Grant a memo describing our little conversation. I am sure he'd be happy to add a copy to your file."

"Leave her alone, Ellen," Jack Ivers said, waving his coffee cup in mock benediction. "For once, let there be peace in our little refuge. Please?"

But Letitia Petrowski, intent on clarifying her position, ignored him.

"I didn't mean anything racial, honest I didn't. I love your people, Ellen. I voted for Obama."

"Uh-huh," Ellen said, sucking her teeth.

The science teacher turned to Bertie with tears in her eyes.

"You know I didn't mean anything by what I said, don't you, Bertie?"

Why do white people always look to me as their ally in these situations? Bertie thought to herself. *Is it because they know I'm a forgiving kind of person, or is it simply that the color of my skin is closer to theirs?* She gave Miss Petrowski an apologetic smile, rinsed her cup out in the sink, and hung it on the peg with her name on it next to the coffeemaker.

"I've got a meeting with Chancellor Grant in five minutes," she said. "See you guys later."

Maria Francione laughed and made the sign of the cross.

"Blessings upon you, my poor child," Francione said as Jack Ivers whistled a chorus of Chopin's *Funeral March.* "May you still be among the gainfully employed when next we meet."

"Pray for me, Your Holiness," Bertie said, not entirely in jest. "I could use all the good vibes I can get."

Walking briskly, Bertie took the elevator to the sixth floor and crossed a glass-enclosed bridge to the newer wing of the campus. Although the building where she taught was dark and smelled faintly of mildew, Metro's new administrative wing was spacious and inviting. Sunlight streamed through the floor to ceiling windows that lined the south wall, and classical music tinkled softly from small speakers hidden discreetly in the ceiling. At an antique desk in the center of this magic kingdom sat Hedda Eberhardt, a.k.a. the Dragon of Doom. As usual, she wore a severe navy-blue suit and matching pumps. As Bertie approached, Eberhardt frowned and looked pointedly at her watch.

"It's three minutes after nine," she said, pointing a perfectly manicured finger in the direction of the chancellor's office. "He's waiting for you inside."

Dr. Humbert Xavier Grant was a portly African American in his mid-sixties. His hair and mustache were gray, as was his suit. A cream-colored, silk handkerchief peeked discreetly from the upper pocket of his jacket. He was sitting at his desk when Bertie walked in. As usual, its surface was completely devoid of clutter. A portrait of Booker T. Washington hung on the wall behind him. Waving his hand imperiously, he gestured for Bertie to sit in the chair facing him.

"You ruined this year's Christmas concert." Dr. Grant spoke in a lugubrious bass reminiscent of James Earl Jones. "You embarrassed the mayor. You embarrassed Alderman Clark. You embarrassed this college, and you embarrassed me. Unless you can provide a satisfactory explanation of this regrettable incident, I will convene a disciplinary hearing and have you censured for professional incompetence."

Fighting back tears, Bertie bit her lip. "I'm terribly sorry. I don't know what got into LaShawn. I can promise you I intend to get to the bottom of it."

"It is way too late for that," Grant snapped. "This boy is nothing but trouble. And now he's been arrested for murder? This is not the kind of student we want here at Metro College."

"Please," Bertie said, "this is not Harvard. It's a community college. Don't we have a mission to help this community? LaShawn is one of the brightest students I've ever had. With a little help, he could really make something of himself."

Dr. Grant raised an eyebrow. "Surely you don't believe the boy is innocent. Not after all the trouble he's caused."

"Of course, I don't know for sure," Bertie said, measuring her words carefully, "but I truly don't believe he would ever shoot anyone."

"Your judgment has not been terribly reliable where this boy is concerned," Grant said grimly. "LaShawn Thomas will be placed on suspension, effective immediately. Once I am satisfied that he poses no danger, he is welcome to return." When Bertie opened her mouth to protest, Dr. Grant held up his hand. "There's no use arguing about this. My decision is final."

He stood up and fixed Bertie with a gimlet eye. "If there is any rational explanation for the behavior of your student at the Christmas concert, you need to get it to me in writing by the end of midterm week. You have sixty days, Professor Bigelow. Are we clear?"

Chapter Eleven

Bertie paced the floor in her office like a trapped animal. Could Dr. Grant really have her reprimanded? She unearthed a dog-eared copy of the Metro College Faculty Handbook from beneath a pile of old papers at the bottom of her desk drawer and turned to page twenty-two:

> **Termination or Suspension of Faculty for Cause:**
> *If the college believes that the behavior of a faculty member poses a sufficiently grave infraction of its code of professional conduct, a hearing of the disciplinary committee may be convened.*

In order to keep from going before the Disciplinary Committee, she was going to have to write the Mother of All Reports justifying her behavior. If she could prove that she had no way of anticipating LaShawn's bizarre outburst, perhaps Dr. Grant would be satisfied to let the matter drop. What on earth had gotten into LaShawn that night? The boy was no murderer, but he had a hell of a lot of explaining to do. Assuming he was released on bond, that is. David Mackenzie had promised to call her the minute he had any news, but as the hours dragged on, Bertie grew more and more restless. It was nearly five o'clock before her phone rang.

"I didn't think I'd be able to pull it off," Mac shouted, his voice breathless with excitement. "For the first ten minutes of the hearing, Judge Dayton lectured me on the moral failings of today's youth. I thought we were done for. But I didn't give up. I argued LaShawn was a good student with no prior record and a grandmother to look after him. In the end, miracle of miracles, Drayton agreed with me."

"So LaShawn is free?" Bertie exhaled deeply for what felt like the first time in three days.

"For the moment," Mac said. "Can you meet us at the Medici in Hyde Park in half an hour? The kid's got something to tell you."

The Medici was an upscale pizza joint popular with Hyde Park locals and students at the nearby University of Chicago. Thirty-five minutes later, Bertie angled her Prius into a semi-legal spot three blocks away from the restaurant. Bracing herself against the biting winter wind, she covered the distance from her car to the Medici in record time. As she walked into the restaurant, Bertie spotted Big Mac and LaShawn Thomas sitting at a table along the brick wall at the back. Sitting next to LaShawn was a stout, dark-skinned woman who was no doubt the boy's grandmother. She wore a hand-knitted hat and a dour expression.

As she approached their table, Mac stood up. "Bertie Bigelow, this is Lurlean Petty, LaShawn's grandmother."

Bertie walked to the table and leaned over to shake the woman's hand.

"It's a pleasure to meet you. I'm the choir director at Metro College."

"I know who you are." Mrs. Petty's lips tightened in an angry line. "You're the one who got my boy the job at that blasted clinic in the first place. If he'd been coming straight home after school like he should have, we wouldn't be sitting here now."

It was true that Bertie had helped LaShawn get his job at the Princeton Natural Health Clinic. She had made similar phone calls on behalf of dozens of students over the years. But this was the first time her well-meaning assistance had ever landed a student in jail.

"Grammie, please" LaShawn mumbled, glancing apologetically in Bertie's direction. "Mrs. B. was just trying to help."

"Umph," Lurlean Petty grunted and turned toward her grandson. "Fine mess of trouble she's gotten you into, LaShawn."

Mac cleared his throat. "I hope you're hungry, folks. I've taken the liberty of ordering us a pizza—deep-dish with all the trimmings."

"I'm starving," Bertie said. "How about you, LaShawn?"

LaShawn shrugged and slouched lower in his seat. Dressed in a ragged black hoodie, baggy jeans, and a pair of unlaced Nikes, he looked like he had not bathed, slept, or eaten in days.

David Mackenzie reached across the table and touched the boy's arm.

"LaShawn has something he wants to tell you. Isn't that right, young man?"

"Yessir," LaShawn said softly, his eyes averted.

"Come on, boy." Lurlean Petty poked her grandson in the side with her elbow. "Out with it."

"I'm sorry about going off like that at the Christmas concert," LaShawn said, continuing to stare down at the table. "I spoiled it for everyone. Like I said before, I'm really, really sorry. When I saw Steady Freddy in the front row, I just lost it, that's all." LaShawn's mouth twisted in an ugly grimace. "Sittin' there all high and mighty, like his shit don't stink."

"What did Alderman Clark ever do to you, LaShawn?" Although Bertie felt her temper flare, she kept her voice gentle. LaShawn was clearly in a fragile state. If she got angry with him now, she'd never find out what had provoked him. "What could possibly justify spoiling the concert like that?"

"He called my father 'worthless trash.' Said he was glad Daddy had been killed. Right on the six o'clock news. You know how many million people watch that stupid show? I know my father had problems, Mrs. B. He was killed in a liquor store hold-up last year. But Steady Freddy Clark had no right to diss him on the news like that. No right at all." On the verge of tears, LaShawn bit his lip hard. "I promised myself I'd get even with that SOB one day. The bastard had it coming."

"As I recall, you called Alderman Clark a junkie," Bertie said. "What was that all about?"

"Look, Mrs. B." The boy's thin fingers drummed nervously on the table. "You're a good person, but there's a lotta stuff you don't know nothin' about."

David Mackenzie grunted. "I've had a very long day, LaShawn. If you don't stop beating around the bush, I'm walking out of here right now."

LaShawn squirmed in his seat, clamped his mouth shut, and resumed his inspection of the tablecloth. Just as the situation appeared to have reached an impasse, their waiter arrived.

"Here you are, people," he said, setting their food on the table with a flourish. "Two large deep-dish pies with the works. Enjoy."

For the next few minutes, silence reigned. The pizza, so thick it had to be eaten with a knife and fork, was gooey, rich, and filling. Bertie, who had been doing her best to watch her diet, fell off the wagon in spectacular fashion, stuffing down two mouth-watering slices in fewer than ten minutes. LaShawn, his eyes fixed greedily on his plate, practically inhaled his pizza. Even Mrs. Petty seemed to unbend a little as she ate. After a suitable interval, Big Mac leaned forward in his seat.

"Alright, LaShawn. Now's the time. I need to know everything you can remember about what happened New Year's Eve."

"Chill out, okay," LaShawn said. "I'm getting to it."

"Mind your manners, boy." Mrs. Petty shot her grandson a threatening glance.

"Sorry, Grammie." LaShawn's angular face flushed deep red. "It's true I went to the judge's apartment that night, but only 'cause they asked me to."

"They?" Mrs. Petty barked. "What 'they' is this? Tell the man the truth, son."

"Mr. Peters at the clinic. He even gave me the gun so I could protect myself if I got held up."

Mac's tone sharpened. "Peters gave you that gun?"

"That's right. Smith & Wesson nine mil." At the look of alarm on his grandmother's face, LaShawn continued hastily. "The cops say it's the murder weapon. That my prints are on it. But I swear, I didn't have the gun that night. Somehow or other I misplaced it."

"*Misplaced?* Don't fool with me, LaShawn," Big Mac snapped. "Judge Green was killed with a gun just like that. Did you or did you not take a gun with you to his apartment?"

LaShawn, trembling and on the brink of tears, shook his head. "No! No! I never did that. The day before the shooting, I left my gun in my sister Sherelle's glove compartment. Somebody broke into her car and stole it. I swear to God that's the truth."

Mac studied LaShawn appraisingly. "It better be, young man. What time was it when you went out to the judge's apartment?"

"Somewhere around one o'clock in the morning, I guess."

"Did anyone see you going in or out?"

LaShawn shrugged. "A couple of people in the elevator, I guess. What difference does it make? I went to his apartment, I handed him the package, and then I left. End of story."

"Whoa. Hold on just a minute, young man." Mac pushed his plate aside and leaned across the table. "There's got to be more, and you know it. What were you doing delivering packages so late at night? What could possibly be so urgent on New Year's Eve that it couldn't wait till morning?"

The minutes passed as LaShawn shifted silently in his seat and stared at the scraps of pizza crust on his plate.

"There's a lotta important people involved in this Testemaxx thing, Mr. Mackenzie. They don't want to have to depend on the mailman, and they *especially* do not want anyone blabbing their business. I'll be in big trouble if I tell."

"You're already in big trouble," Mac said grimly. "The police report says you delivered bottles of Testemaxx late at night on a regular basis to several city officials. Is this true?"

LaShawn shook his head. "They must have misheard me. I never said nothing 'bout that."

"Is that why you called the Alderman a junkie at the Christmas concert?" Bertie said. "Because he was using Testemaxx?"

LaShawn smirked. "The man's a phony, Mrs. B. That's all I'm sayin'."

"This is no laughing matter," Bertie snapped. "Dr. Grant has given me sixty days to explain what happened at the concert or else I'll be officially censured. And if that doesn't get your attention, think about this—the college has put you on suspension. You are not allowed to set one foot on campus until this is cleared up. Don't you want to graduate?"

"I'm sorry, Mrs. B. I'm sorry about everything," LaShawn said, his lower lip trembling. "But I didn't kill the judge. I'm *innocent*. I can prove it."

Mac shook his head wearily. "Life is no video game, son. If you've got anything more to tell me, now's the time."

"No, Mr. Mackenzie. You can't help me." LaShawn stood up and pulled on a battered Bulls jacket. "I've got to do this myself." Without waiting for a reply, he ran out of the restaurant, banging the door behind him.

"Looks like we've come to the end of the road," Mrs. Petty said, gathering up her coat. "I know you're tryin' to help, Mrs. Bigelow. But the way I see it, your meddling has landed my boy in a world of trouble."

"LaShawn does a good job of finding trouble on his own," Mac said drily. He signaled for the waiter to bring the check. "Whatever you do, don't let him go back to school until this thing has been resolved. If he's arrested for trespassing, Judge Drayton could decide to put him back in jail."

Mrs. Petty sighed heavily and sat back down. In that moment she looked old, frail, and very vulnerable.

"I sure was looking forward to graduation this spring," she said softly. "LaShawn was gonna be the first person in our family to ever finish college."

"It's only January," Bertie said. "If we can convince Dr. Grant of LaShawn's innocence in the next few weeks, there's a chance he could still graduate."

Mrs. Petty nodded glumly.

"Now that LaShawn's been released on bail, I'll talk to Dr. Grant again. I will do what I can to help him get reinstated."

"I'm going to hold you to that promise, Mrs. Bigelow."

With a curt nod, Lurlean Petty stood up, wrapped a thick scarf tightly around her face, and walked out.

Chapter Twelve

LaShawn's suspension was the hot topic on campus when Bertie arrived at work. In the hallways, students clustered in little knots, arguing about whether Dr. Grant had done the right thing. Over coffee in the faculty lounge, Jack Ivers treated his colleagues to a blistering tirade. Although he detested LaShawn Thomas as a person, this was a matter of principle.

"This is America, not Communist China. A man is presumed innocent until proven guilty," Ivers thundered. "This college is in violation of fundamental constitutional principles." In a rare moment of collegial unity, Ellen Simpson agreed.

By Tuesday morning, the two teachers were circulating a petition demanding LaShawn's reinstatement.

"It's important to be vigilant," Ellen said, her eyes flashing. Perched on the corner of the desk in Bertie's office, she waved her coffee cup to emphasize the point. "If we aren't vigilant in the little things, the big things will catch us unawares. Take the Muslims, for example."

"I'd rather not," Bertie said, sighing inwardly. When Ellen went off on a tear on a political issue like this, there was no stopping her.

"Since 9/11 our government has been persecuting the Muslims relentlessly—tapping their phones, following them," Ellen said. "All this despite overwhelming evidence that the vast majority of Muslims are law-abiding tax payers, just like the rest of us."

"True," Bertie said. "But what does this have to do with LaShawn being kicked out of school?"

"It's a matter of principle, Bertie. *Principle.*" Ellen stood up and began pacing back and forth as her lecture gathered steam. "In America, every man is presumed innocent until a court of law finds him guilty. The first time this happened to someone I knew, I was too young to stop it. Things are different this time around."

"Sit down," Bertie said. "You're making me dizzy. What do you mean, this time around? Has LaShawn been kicked out of school before?"

"I'm not talking about LaShawn, Bertie. I'm talking about Raquib Torrence. Didn't I ever tell you about him?"

After resuming her perch on the edge of Bertie's desk, Ellen recounted the story of her long-ago romance with a tall, dark, and fiercely activist brother from Texas. During her sophomore year at Harvard, Raquib had wooed her with flowers, love songs, and rhetoric. The sex had been as hot as their politics, and for a while in the mid-nineties, Ellen had given serious thought to becoming Mrs. Raquib Torrence.

"So what happened?" Bertie said. "Sounds like the two of you would have been quite the power couple."

"Raquib changed his last name to Kujamiiana."

"So?"

Ellen shot her a pitying look. "You really need to brush up on your African phrases, Bertie. Kujamiiana means 'virile' in Swahili."

"Sounds like a good thing to me," Bertie said.

"Man was a bit too virile for his own good," Ellen said. "He joined a Muslim splinter group and took on five common-law wives. Needless to say, we broke up. Rumor has it he moved back to Texas to start his own church—The Mosque of the Mighty Black Sword."

"Not hard to find the metaphor in that title," Bertie said drily.

"Hard was the operative term," Ellen said. "The man was a sexist idiot—a Neanderthal, really. But one thing's for sure. The brother could take care of business between the sheets." She sighed. "You remember that song R. Kelly used to sing? 'Bump N' Grind'? Girl, we wore that record *out*."

"Ever thought about reconnecting? You could probably find him on Facebook or something."

"You know I'm computer phobic," Ellen said, laughing.

"You want me to look him up for you? I'm kind of curious what he looks like."

"Hell, no. It's been nearly twenty years. Seeing him with a bald head and a potbelly is going to spoil the romance completely." Ellen drained the last of her coffee and stood up. "Speaking of romance, I'm going to give you a little unsolicited advice, Bertie. It's time you to started dating again. David Mackenzie's got the hots for you." She winked and ground her hips suggestively. "I know you had a rough go with Theophilous. But as the old saying goes, the best thing to do after you've fallen off a horse is to jump back on and ride."

As Bertie walked down the hall to her next class, she thought about Ellen's comment. A shy and private person when she was not performing, Bertie envied Ellen's confident sexuality. But Delroy had only been gone nine months. It was way too soon to even be thinking about kissing any other man. Still, if she was really honest with herself, Bertie could not deny the facts. Like it or not, her pulse had quickened when Big Mac had placed his hand over hers. It had been on the tip of her tongue to tell Ellen about the gesture, but she'd thought better of it in the nick of time. It had been over a decade since Bertie had flirted with a man. It was entirely possible she'd gotten her signals crossed. Most likely Mac had intended his touch to be purely platonic. Anyway, she reminded herself for the tenth time that day, David Mackenzie was a married man.

Chapter Thirteen

For the rest of the week, Bertie scoured *ChicagoTribune.com* for news of a breakthrough in the case. But there were no new developments, and by Thursday, Judge Green's murder had faded from the headlines completely. In the midst of all this drama, an entire week of classes went by in a blur. Bertie had lesson plans to complete, exams to prepare, and essays to grade. The music theater club had decided to do *The Wiz* in the spring, and between holding tryouts for the lead roles and negotiating an affordable price for the performance rights, Bertie had her hands full. By the time she got home from work Friday afternoon, she was ready to relax in front of the TV with a glass of wine and a large bowl of popcorn.

Five minutes after she walked in the door, her neighbor Colleen O'Fallon rang the doorbell.

"You'll be goin' to the festivities, I'm assuming," O'Fallon chirped, her pale cheeks flush with excitement.

"What festivities?" Bertie gestured for the gnome-like woman to step inside. "I just this minute got home from work."

"A course ya did, dear. Me and Pat, we watched ya drive up. We've been waitin' for hours." Colleen O'Fallon pulled a shiny red piece of paper from her pocket and thrust it in Bertie's face. "Will ya be attendin'?"

Bertie took the paper and studied it:

CHARLEY HOWARD'S HOT LINK EMPORIUM
The Best in Southern Cuisine
3473 South Prairie Avenue

GRAND OPENING—TONIGHT ONLY
PRIZES
LIVE ENTERTAINMENT
PATRONS WITH ORDERS OF $25 OR MORE
WILL RECEIVE A FREE BOTTLE OF
HOWARD'S HEAVENLY HOT SAUCE WITH OUR
COMPLIMENTS

"Pat said you'd be too worn ta go," Colleen said. "I told her she was wrong, dead wrong. It's concernin' Bertie's favorite food, I told her. A-course she'll go, I said. It's inevitable."

As she studied Charley Howard's flyer, Bertie remembered the bitter argument she'd witnessed between Howard and Judge Green at the Octagon Ball. Could the Hot Sauce King have been angry enough with Theophilous to shoot him in cold blood?

As Bertie continued to study the flyer, Colleen O'Fallon shifted from one foot to the other in a lather of excitement.

"Now then," she said. "Was I right? Will ya be attendin'?"

"Definitely," Bertie said with a smile. "You might say Charley Howard and I are friends."

"I *knew* it. Wait till I tell that know-it-all sister of mine." Colleen O'Fallon lifted her clasped fists in triumph over her head. "Oh. And if it's not a terrible bother, d'ya mind bringing me a bottle of that hot sauce? Grand stuff, that."

Twenty minutes later, Bertie was standing in front of Howard's Hot Link Emporium. The worn brick tenement that housed the restaurant had been painted fire-engine red, and New Orleans jazz poured from two oversized speakers mounted over the entrance. On the sidewalk in front of the building, shivering waitresses dressed in sequined Mardi Gras outfits distributed bottles of Heavenly Hot Sauce to curious passersby. Taking her place at the end of the long line of customers waiting for a table, Bertie reviewed her hastily devised game plan. The goal was to find Charley Howard, chat him up a little, and get him to talk about the argument he'd had with Judge Green. Bertie figured the Hot Sauce King would be a lot more likely to let his guard down with her than with the police. With any luck, he'd slip up and say something incriminating. Once that happened, Bertie would inform Dr. Grant and *voila!* LaShawn would be in the clear. He'd be able to return to school, rejoin the choir, and graduate in the spring.

When Bertie finally got to the head of the line, she spotted the Hot Sauce King mixing drinks at the bar. Squeezing quickly past a harried mother and her three hungry toddlers, Bertie made her way across the restaurant. Pasting a genial, nonthreatening expression on her face, Bertie slid onto an empty bar stool and waved until she caught Howard's attention.

"What a nice surprise!" the Hot Sauce King boomed. Resplendent in a pair of blue overalls, a red-and-white checked shirt, and a white chef's hat, he wiped the bar down with a wet rag and slid a coaster in front of her. "What can I do ya for?"

Bertie ordered a glass of merlot and congratulated Howard on the success of his new restaurant.

"Tell you the truth, I'm right pleased." Howard pulled a large, red handkerchief from the rear pocket of his overalls and mopped his brow. "Twenty thirteen is gonna be a banner year for me, Bertie. I've been accepted into the Octagon Society. Mrs. Leflore's gonna send out the official announcement next week."

"Congratulations, Charley," Bertie said, raising her glass. "Mind if I ask you what changed her mind? Last time I heard, you weren't exactly a shoo-in."

Howard's laugh was hearty. "You're right about that, darlin'. Once Judge Green was out of the picture, Mrs. Leflore was quick to come 'round to my way of thinking. Not that I wished the old bastard any harm, of course."

"Of course not," Bertie said. "You've got to admit it was convenient, though. Theophilous kicking the bucket the way he did."

"Damn convenient." Placing both elbows on the bar, the Hot Sauce King leaned in close. "I know you think I'm some kind of thug, Bertie. But I didn't kill that old man. And in case you're wondering, I didn't get the Roselli boys to knock him off, either. Truth is, I'm a peaceful man once you get to know me."

There was only one more piece of information Bertie hoped to acquire. To get it, she was going to have to catch Charley Howard by surprise.

"I would hardly describe breaking someone's nose as the actions of a peaceful man," Bertie said, smiling her sweetest smile. "Would you?"

Howard's eyes narrowed. "What the hell are you talkin' about?"

"I'm talking about Mr. Elmer Jones," Bertie said, pleased she'd taken a minute to review the thumbnail sketch of Howard in Delroy's manuscript before coming to the restaurant. "The chairman of the board at your condo, remember? He made fun of your down-home accent. He said his property values would go down if you moved in. According to the police, you weren't too peaceful with him."

"That was nearly twenty years ago. It was a mistake. All the charges against me were dropped." Howard spread his hands open on the bar and smiled through clenched teeth. "I'm telling you, I'm a peaceful man. Just ask anybody."

"I was there when you got into it with Judge Green at the gala," Bertie persisted. "I would hardly describe your demeanor as peaceful. Did you stop by the judge's place later that night to continue the discussion?"

"Out!" the Hot Sauce King growled. "If it's one thing I can't stand, it's a busybody."

He snatched Bertie's half-full glass of merlot off the bar and emptied it into the sink. As she stood up to leave, Bertie could not resist a parting shot.

"Have you something to hide, Charley? Why won't you tell me where you went after the gala?"

"I don't *have* to say a goddamn thing," Howard said. "But just to keep you from spreading false rumors, I will. After the gala, my wife and I went to see Mrs. Leflore."

Bertie raised her eyebrows. "Doesn't she live in Jackson Towers?"

"Shaw 'nuff, Miz Nosey Parker," Charley Howard drawled sarcastically. "While Judge Green was getting himself shot, the wife and I were sitting two floors up, discussing my contribution to the Scholarship Fund." He looked at Bertie and flashed a nasty grin. "Satisfied?"

Chapter Fourteen

Bertie awoke the next morning with a churning stomach and a head full of worries. What had she been thinking, baiting Charley Howard like that? If the Hot Sauce King was half as dangerous as he was reputed to be, he could be ordering her execution this very minute. Who the hell did she think she was, anyway? That crazy white woman on *Murder, She Wrote*?

Bertie draped a pink cotton bathrobe over her shoulders, padded into the kitchen, and brewed herself a strong cup of tea. It was snowing, and from the looks of things, there would be at least four more inches of the white stuff on the ground by midafternoon. Cup in hand, she leafed idly through the music books piled precariously next to the baby grand piano that dominated her living room. Digging the music for Bach's *Partitas for Solo Piano* out of the pile, Bertie sat down at the piano bench, lifted the instrument's wooden cover, and ran her fingers gently over the keys. Almost instantly, Bertie felt the worries and irritations of the past few days dissolve. Soon there was only *music*—a universe where every note, no matter how dissonant, found its resolution in an orderly architecture of sound and silence, tension and release.

But halfway through the second movement of the *Partita in D minor*, a voice nagged at the back of Bertie's mind. *What on earth was the matter with LaShawn, storming out of the restaurant like that?* With renewed determination, Bertie plunged into her practice routine, working through the difficult passages slowly, one hand at a time. Once all the details were mastered, the Partita would become as easy to play as "Chopsticks." But try as she might, speculations about the murder continued to intrude.

I'm innocent, the boy said. *And I can prove it.*

Bertie got up from the piano bench, closed the lid, and plopped down on her living room couch in a funk. Before his meltdown at the Christmas concert, LaShawn Thomas had been her most promising student. It would be a terrible shame if he had to leave Metro just one semester shy of graduation. Still, the police had found his prints on the murder weapon. Was she being foolish to believe in his innocence?

Wonder what Delroy would say about all this, she thought to herself. As she glanced around the room, her eye fell on the three yellow legal pads on the coffee table in front of her. Though Delroy was gone, he had left her this manuscript. She'd already gleaned some valuable clues from it. Alderman Clark cheating on a test in college. Charley Howard's arrest record. Dr. Taylor's African harem. Maybe if she read it again, Bertie thought to herself, maybe she would spot something she'd missed the first time around. Something that would help her identify the real killer and clear LaShawn's name.

While she ate breakfast, she idly flipped through the legal pad that contained the third section of her husband's memoir until she came to Judge Green's comments on the last page.

Re: Actionable nature of MS: Verify all docs—birth certs., crim. hist., citizenshp papers, etc. Re-depose before pub.—audi alteram partem!

Why couldn't Judge Green have written his thoughts in plain English? What's more, why hadn't he returned the manuscript to her immediately after her husband's death? Had Theophilous just forgotten about it, or had he held onto the manuscript because of something Delroy had written? Frustrated, Bertie pushed the legal pads aside and went into the kitchen to put the kettle on. As she sipped her tea, she watched the snow pile up on the street outside. A thick, heavy blanket of the white stuff covered the cars, the street, and the sidewalk in front of her house. Although it was normally fairly busy on Harper Avenue, not a soul passed in front of her window.

Feeling somewhat at loose ends, she drifted back into the living room and sat down on the couch. *Come on, Bertie. Use your noggin.* Her late husband had loved that phrase. Whenever Delroy felt she was missing something, he'd teased her with it. *Use your noggin, Bertie.*

Maybe she'd never be able to know for sure why Theophilous had kept the manuscript so long. But at least she could try to decipher the comments he'd written. The judge had been concerned about Delroy being sued for libel because of something in his manuscript. That's what he'd meant by "actionable." Okay, so far so good. What exactly had concerned the judge? The first thing he'd told Delroy to do was to "verify all docs." That made sense. Although not meant as a muckraker, Delroy's memoir would reveal the hidden sides of some of the most well-known African Americans in Chicago. To avoid a lawsuit, Delroy would have needed to back up every allegation with solid evidence.

The judge's injunction to "Re-depose before pub." also began to make sense. He was suggesting Delroy question his subjects again, giving them each a chance to respond to what he'd written before publication. After all, Karen Phillips's fudged birth dates, Charley Howard's arrest record, Dr. Taylor's questionable claim of kinship with the wealthy Henries family in Liberia, and Silas Blackstone's illegitimate child would become public knowledge once the book was published.

David Mackenzie had told her *Audi alteram partem* was Latin for "hear from the other side." Had her late husband actually done this? The Lord had taken her Delroy away in the middle of a very busy life. His old study downstairs was filled with boxes of papers and files she had yet to sort through. Every weekend for the last couple of months, she had promised herself she would clean out the room, but every weekend she found an excuse not to. Sometimes she'd even get all the way down to the door before suddenly "remembering" an urgent appointment to do something else. Pensively, Bertie took another sip of tea. The snow outside continued to pile up. Not a single car was moving outside her window.

I've been talking about going through that stuff downstairs for months. Now's as good a time as any. Who knows? Maybe there's a clue buried in Delroy's papers somewhere.

Delroy's study was in the basement—more of a glorified closet than a room, really. Jammed against the back wall was a small desk piled high with papers. On the wall above the desk hung his African mask collection. Hand carved from ebony and decorated with raffia, beads, and cowrie shells, the masks had cost a small fortune. When Bertie had teased him about the expense, Delroy had grown uncharacteristically serious.

"My Caucasian friends can trace their families back to England or Ireland or wherever. I will never know for sure exactly where I come from. I just need to own a little piece of *my* mother country."

Bookshelves lined the walls on each side of the room. Easy Rollins murder mysteries sat cheek to jowl with Plato's *Republic*. Kevin Shillington's three-volume *Encyclopedia of African History*, a signed copy of *Roots*, and a tattered paperback edition of *The Souls of Black Folk* by W.E. B. DuBois. Most of the available floor space was covered with boxes stacked in teetering piles. At the sight of all the clutter and confusion, it took all of Bertie's willpower not to turn and run. The room even smelled faintly of the pipe her late husband had smoked in the evenings after dinner. Feeling her eyes begin to fill with tears, Bertie bit her lip hard. Now that she'd finally made herself come down here, Bertie was determined not to become sidetracked by grief. After two hours of determined digging, she uncovered a large cardboard box labeled *BOOK RESEARCH.*

Clearing herself a space on the floor, Bertie removed the stack of manila file folders from the box and piled them up next to her. Contained in the files were photocopies of legal documents—birth and death certificates, incorporation papers, naturalization papers, motions filed and counter-filed. Was there anything in the files that might explain the judge's cryptic comments? Though Bertie knew it wasn't likely, anything was possible. Carefully gathering up all the papers, she returned them to the box and carried it back upstairs.

When she returned to the living room, it was nearly six o'clock. She'd been down in the basement much longer than she'd realized. Fortunately, it had stopped snowing. The city looked deceptively peaceful in its blanket of white. The O'Fallon sisters were already out clearing their sidewalks, the scraping of their shovels strangely muffled by the snow.

Looks like I'll be snowed in this evening, Bertie said to herself. *I'll fix myself some dinner and then take a look at these files.*

As she pulled her Weight Watcher's TV dinner out of the oven, the phone rang.

"Hey, girl," Ellen's voice sounded unusually loud in Bertie's ear after spending the day alone. "Aren't you sick of being cooped up inside? My new friend Jerome and I are going to The Loft to hear some jazz. We'll be in front of your house in an hour. Don't even think about saying no."

Chapter Fifteen

Despite the snow and the cold outside, The Loft was jumping. Patrons wearing everything from hoodies to full-length fur coats lined the large circular bar in the center of the club. At the opposite end of the room, Earl Mallory's group was deep into their first set.

"Guess we're not the only people with cabin fever," Ellen shouted over the din of the music. She tapped Jerome on the shoulder. "Bertie and I will go find a table while you get the drinks, okay, honey?"

Jerome, a lean man in his early forties with a shaved head and a diamond stud in his left ear, nodded and waded into the crowd huddled around the bar.

Fortunately for Bertie, there were still a couple of empty tables near the stage. Slipping out of her coat, she flashed Ellen an appreciative smile. *What a blessing it is to have friends. If Ellen hadn't called, I would have stayed home brooding all night, for sure.* For the next several minutes, Bertie immersed herself in the music. Now in his mid-eighties, Earl Mallory was a Chicago legend who'd cut his teeth performing with the Count Basie Orchestra before going on to form his own group.

Improbably, Mallory was playing better than ever. Energy poured from the bell of his tenor sax, challenging his audience to abandon their conversations and focus in on the music. Warming herself with an occasional sip from a shot of Hennessy, Bertie closed her eyes and listened, delighting in the complex interplay between Mallory's horn and the guitar, bass, and drums that accompanied him. Geometric designs in bright colors flashed through her mind as she listened—each note a new shade of red, blue, purple, and orange. A beautiful mosaic of sights and sounds.

"Bertie . . . *Bertie!*" The sharp sensation of Ellen's elbow poking into her ribs jarred her from her reverie. "Don't look now, but I think I just saw Patrice Soule."

"Who?" Intent on the rhythm unfolding in Mallory's sax solo, Bertie barely acknowledged her friend's comment.

"Patrice Soule. You know, the hot new singer who won the Illinois Idol contest last year." Ellen leaned closer so Bertie could hear her over the music. "And you'll never guess who's with her."

"Dr. Taylor," Bertie said in a matter-of-fact tone. "They went to the Octagon Gala together. Didn't I tell you?"

"You most definitely did not, girlfriend. I would have remembered something like that. When Patrice Soule won the Idol contest, I cried my eyes out. Local girl makes good. Great stuff. Wonder what she sees in Dr. Taylor. The man's old enough to be her father."

Eager to get back to the music, Bertie shrugged. Ellen, however, could not let the matter go.

"That's what's wrong with our society today, Bert. A man can be old as Methuselah and still keep a beautiful woman on his arm. If a woman did that, everybody'd be talking 'bout how the dude was just a boy toy or, worse yet, a paid gigolo."

"What difference does it make?" Sneaking a glance to make sure Jerome wasn't listening, Bertie leaned closer to Ellen and whispered, "After all, I see you've got yourself a fine young thing of your own. Where do you find them, Ellen? This is the handsomest one yet."

"My cousin Charles introduced us," Ellen said. She clinked her glass against Bertie's and winked. "Just don't tell him my real age, okay?"

Bertie giggled. "Mum's the word, I promise."

Earl Mallory concluded his first set with a dazzling blues number that showcased each member of the band in turn. As the audience clapped and whistled their approval, Mallory smiled and took a bow.

"We're gonna take a brief pause for the cause," he announced. "Don't go nowhere, folks. We're coming right back."

The minute the band stopped playing, Bertie went off in search of the ladies room only to discover that half the women in the audience had similar plans. The bathroom line stretched well past the bar and showed no sign of moving. Discouraged, she took a seat at the bar to wait. To keep herself company, Bertie ordered another brandy and swiveled her high-backed leather stool around for a better view of the club.

It was a typical South Side crowd—hardworking black folks determined to squeeze the last drop of pleasure from the weekend before returning to work on Monday. Women strutted their stuff in tightfitting dresses and heels while the men enjoyed the show, gazing in frank appreciation as the ladies shimmied by. From atop her barstool, Bertie watched as Jerome slipped his arm around Ellen's shoulders and pulled her close. It would be nice if this man were serious about Ellen, she thought. Though she missed Delroy terribly, at least they'd had ten wonderful years together. Everybody deserved to enjoy true love at least once in his life.

"Bertie Bigelow. What a pleasant surprise." Placing a hand on her shoulder, Dr. Momolu Taylor bent down and kissed her cheek. "I wouldn't have expected you to be out on such a foul night."

"I have to say, I'm somewhat surprised myself," Bertie said. "My friend Ellen is entirely responsible for getting me out of the house." Taylor turned his head to look as Bertie pointed to where Ellen sat, gazing soulfully into Jerome's eyes.

"Your friend looks a bit busy at the moment," Taylor said. "Perhaps you'd like to join my friends and me for a quick drink?"

After gesturing to the bartender to bring another round of drinks to his table, the doctor offered Bertie his arm. Perhaps it was the two shots of Hennessy she'd consumed, but Bertie had the distinct feeling of being weightless, disconnected from gravity as she floated across the room toward Taylor's table. As she approached, she could see Patrice Soule—stunning in a low-cut silk blouse, formfitting red miniskirt, and expensive Italian boots—fiddle restlessly with her iPhone.

"It's a pleasure to meet you, Miss Soule," Bertie said. "I heard you sing at the Octagon Gala."

With a tiny frown, Soule put down her phone.

"I hadn't planned on doing anything, but Mrs. Leflore asked me. What else could I do?" Clearly the diva was a bit put off at being approached by yet another fan. It probably happened all the time, especially since winning the Illinois Idol contest two years ago. On the other hand, there was nothing any diva loved better than flattery.

"You handled the situation beautifully," Bertie said. "I loved the way you reworked the original melody."

"Did I change it?" Soule giggled. "I just sing the song how I feel it, so it's different every time. I can't read a note of music, you know. Drives my piano players nuts."

"Reading music is a lot easier than it looks," Bertie said. "I've taught hundreds of people how to do it. I could probably show you in a couple of hours."

"Really?" Trembling with excitement, Soule clapped her hands together like a small child. "Did you hear that? Professor Bigelow is going to tutor me."

Dr. Taylor raised an eyebrow. "You'll need a lot of patience, eh? Patrice's last tutor didn't last a single week."

"Momo, *please!*"

Ignoring Soule, Taylor gestured toward the bald, heavyset man sitting on the other side of the table. "Bertie, this is Jawann Peters, the assistant director at my clinic."

When she shook his hand, Bertie couldn't help thinking that Peters, dressed in a black-and-red track suit and sporting a diamond pinkie ring, looked a lot more like a hoodlum than a medical administrator.

"Seriously, Momo. My last tutor treated me like I was some kind of idiot," Patrice cut in, her voice rising. "I may not be able to read music, but I'm no moron."

"Of course not, darling," Taylor said. He looked over at Peters and winked. "Any man with a pulse can see you're a young woman overflowing with talent."

Patrice Soule stuck out her tongue, lifted her glass, and emptied it in one long swallow.

"Would you mind fetching me another rum and Coke, Jawann dear? I'm feeling awful thirsty tonight."

After the tiniest of nods from the doctor, Peters pushed back from the table and lumbered off toward the bar. Taylor gestured for Bertie to take a seat in the chair next to his.

"Your late husband was somewhat of a mentor to me," he said. "I admired him deeply, at least in part because he had the good fortune to be married to such a beautiful woman." Leaning so close Bertie could smell the musk in his aftershave, Taylor whispered, "Now that you're single, perhaps we could spend some time together."

Bertie felt her skin flush. Did the doctor flirt like this with every woman he met? *I really ought to get up and walk away,* she told herself. Instead, her senses dulled by the lateness of the hour and the liquor she'd consumed, Bertie merely smiled.

"Oh, I'm sure we're both too busy for anything like that, Dr. Taylor," she said, taking a covert look toward Patrice Soule to see whether the diva had noticed Taylor coming on to her. Fortunately, Soule was once again tapping into her phone, oblivious to the world around her. *Probably chatting with her fans on Twitter,* Bertie thought to herself.

"When I was trying to open my clinic five years ago, Bill Hedgegrave called me an 'ignorant voodoo witch doctor' on WLS radio." Edging his chair closer, Taylor squeezed Bertie on the arm. "The city did not want to grant me a license, but your husband sued the station for libel and won."

"I know," Bertie said. "Delroy wrote a chapter in his memoir about it."

"Really? I had no idea he'd written anything." Bertie couldn't be completely sure, but she thought she felt Taylor's grip on her arm tighten.

"Neither did I until Judge Green showed me the manuscript. I'm thinking of trying to find a publisher for the thing."

"How interesting," Taylor purred. Though his voice remained as smooth as ever, Bertie was absolutely certain Taylor was squeezing her arm harder than before.

"I need to clear up a few loose ends before it can be published," she said. "I don't know why, but Judge Green wanted Delroy to recheck all his documentation."

A strange expression flitted across the doctor's face. But before Bertie could figure out what it meant, he was smiling again.

"That sounds like Theophilous. Not to speak ill of the dead, but the old man was a bit off his rocker, I'm afraid." Releasing his grip on Bertie's arm, the doctor lifted his highball and nodded in Soule's direction. "Baby, tell Bertie what Judge Green said to you."

"Which time? The man was completely paranoid. One time, he told me Charley Howard was part of a Mafia plot to destroy the Octagon Society. Another time, he told me Steady Freddy Clark was selling drugs for the CIA." Soule laughed and twirled an elegantly manicured index finger in circles around her ear. "The man was a total fruitcake. I didn't mind the paranoia so much until he started following me around the building. One night when I was in the laundry room alone, he even tried to kiss me."

Bertie raised an eyebrow. "Did he do that sort of thing a lot?"

"Not after I showed him my gun. Smith & Wesson nine mil. Told him if he ever did it again, I'd blow his ass to kingdom come."

"Looks like somebody else had the same idea. Unless, of course, it was you."

Soule's face reddened. "You're kidding, right?"

Taylor laughed and squeezed Soule's thigh. "Of course she is, sugar. For the record, I was with Ms. Soule on the night the judge was killed, Miss Prosecutor. Just the two of us, alone in her apartment. And a magnum of Champagne to keep us company."

Jawann Peters had been knocking back shots of Johnnie Walker Black as he followed the conversation.

"With all due respect, Bertie," he said in a gravelly voice. "You of all people should know who really shot the judge. You're the one who suggested I hire LaShawn Thomas in the first place."

Bertie's face reddened. "I thought LaShawn was a good kid when I wrote his reference letter, and I still think so now. You're the one who gave him that gun. Don't you feel any responsibility for what happened?"

"I certainly didn't expect him to kill innocent people with it, if that's what you're thinking."

"Jawann was just trying to help the boy," Taylor interjected smoothly. "Englewood's a tough neighborhood."

"What was in those packages, anyway? LaShawn says it was some kind of hormone enhancer," Bertie said. "Is that true?"

The doctor's laugh was as melodious as his speaking voice.

"I'd asked him to not to tell anyone. But since you already know my little secret, I'll explain." His eyes sparkled with excitement. "I've invented a new formula for improving male sexual performance. Testamaxx contains an herbal aphrodisiac that men in Liberia have been using successfully for hundreds of years. My grandfather, Togar Momolu Henries, was a Mandinka chief. With the help of this formula, the man produced thirty-one children." Standing up, Taylor spread his arms wide in a grand gesture and intoned, "Testemaxx—the perfect marriage of African wisdom and Western science. It will revolutionize the world!"

With a giddy shriek of excitement, Patrice Soule tossed off the remainder of her drink, stood up, and launched into a pitch perfect imitation of Aretha Franklin's "Dr. Feelgood."

After finishing up with a soaring riff, Soule wrapped her arms around the doctor and planted a juicy kiss on his mouth. As the diva waved gaily to the growing crowd of people surrounding them, the doctor reddened and returned to his seat. When Soule launched into a second chorus of "Dr. Feelgood," Taylor grabbed her roughly by the wrist and pulled her down.

"Shut up, Patrice," he hissed. "You're embarrassing me."

Landing heavily in her seat, the diva bit her lip, grabbed her iPhone, and resumed tapping into it furiously. In the awkward silence that followed, Bertie pushed back her chair.

"My friends must be wondering what happened to me," she said, extracting a business card from her purse. "Patrice, if you ever want me to help you with your music reading, give me a call."

In the car on the way home, Bertie couldn't shake the feeling that she'd stepped in the middle of something ugly between Patrice Soule and Dr. Taylor.

"The vibes at their table were really off-key," she said. "You could cut the tension with a knife."

"Don't be so melodramatic," Ellen said. As Jerome shifted her aging Volvo into second gear, she leaned over and nibbled his ear. "The doctor is just your typical alpha male, obsessed with being in control of every situation. He got upset because Soule embarrassed him. You know how men are."

"Not me, babe." Jerome said, stroking Ellen's cheek with his free hand. "Long as you keep givin' me the love I need, you can embarrass me whenever you want."

"Hey, baby," Ellen said, resting her head on his shoulder, "let's go home and put R. Kelly on the stereo."

Feeling more than a little in the way, Bertie turned and looked out the window. Between the bumpy road, the overheated car, and all the brandy she'd consumed, her stomach felt decidedly woozy. After Ellen dropped her off, she barely made it into the living room before collapsing in a heap on the couch.

If Delroy had been with her, he would have picked her up and carried her upstairs. Of course, if Delroy had been with her, Bertie would not have drunk that much brandy in the first place. And certainly, if Delroy had been with her, she would never have sat at the doctor's table and let him flirt with her like that.

But Delroy was not with her. Delroy would never be with her again. She was a widow now—destined to walk a treacherous path filled with unscripted social interactions and saturated with loneliness. Willing herself up the stairs, Bertie Bigelow stripped off her clothes, burrowed under the covers, and cried herself to sleep.

Chapter Sixteen

When Bertie arrived at work Monday morning, she found Hedda Eberhardt waiting in the hallway. Catching Bertie's eye, the chancellor's secretary waved imperiously and began walking toward the elevator.

"Hurry up," Eberhardt said over her shoulder. "Dr. Grant is waiting upstairs. Alderman Clark wants to talk to you."

As she struggled to keep up, Bertie's thoughts whirled furiously. Why would Alderman Clark want to see her at eight thirty on a Monday morning? In fact, why would Alderman Clark want to see her at all?

As they entered the administrative wing, Bertie was surprised to see a small crowd of students standing in the reception area. Dressed identically in black jeans and hoodies, they stood silently, holding aloft homemade signs. *Bring LaShawn Back!* read one. More ominously, another proclaimed, *Down with Dictators—Give Grant the Boot.*

With an irritated shake of her head, Hedda Eberhardt pushed past the demonstrators and knocked on the door to Dr. Grant's office. After a brief pause, she gestured for Bertie to go inside. Seated in the two leather armchairs facing Grant's large picture window, Grant and Steady Freddy Clark were in the midst of what appeared to be an intense conversation. Alderman Clark's handsome brown face was twisted in an uncharacteristic grimace, and his index finger was pointed straight at Dr. Grant's face.

Uh-oh, Bertie thought to herself. *Whatever is going on here does not look good, not at all.* Taking a deep breath, she stepped farther into the room and cleared her throat.

"Good morning, gentlemen. Hedda Eberhardt said you wanted to see me, so I came right up. As you can see, I didn't even stop in my office to hang up my coat."

At the sound of Bertie's voice, the two men stood up.

"A pleasure to meet you, Professor Bigelow." As usual, the alderman exuded an air of confidence. If the discussion he and Grant had been having had rattled Steady Freddy, he didn't show it. Nor did he make any reference to the protest taking place outside the office. As usual, the alderman was well dressed, this time in a charcoal Brooks Brothers suit. A faint hint of expensive cologne emanated from his body.

"I so enjoyed the music your choir performed at the Christmas concert," he said, taking Bertie's hand and pressing it between his own. "Dr. Grant assures me that you were as surprised as the rest of us when the unfortunate incident occurred."

"Absolutely," Bertie said, shaking the alderman's manicured hand vigorously. "On behalf of all my students, I would like to apologize for LaShawn's remarks. The whole situation has been a terrible embarrassment."

The alderman's booming laugh filled the room. "When you've been on the campaign trail as often as I have, you learn that there's just no predicting what some people will do to get attention. Isn't that right, Humbert?"

"Have a seat, Professor Bigelow," Dr. Grant said. "We were just about to have coffee."

Dutifully, Bertie took a seat on the black leather couch facing the two men. Moments later, Hedda Eberhardt appeared, carrying a tray of small breakfast pastries and a large metal coffee pot. Once the coffee had been poured and the pastries distributed, she withdrew, her feet soundless on the plush, beige carpet.

"The alderman would like your choir to perform at his campaign rally next month," Dr. Grant said, wiping his hands delicately with a paper napkin.

"We'd be happy to do that," Bertie said.

Steady Freddy Clark rubbed his hands together and exchanged a look with the chancellor.

"I had hoped that LaShawn Thomas would be able to participate, but I've been informed he's been placed on suspension."

"You wanted LaShawn to sing?" Suddenly flustered, Bertie groped to find the right words. "We both saw what happened the last time he got near a microphone."

"That's exactly my point," Steady Freddy said, beaming his fifty-megawatt smile. "Nearly half the voters in my district are under thirty. To them, LaShawn has become something of a celebrity. Now that he's suspected of murder, sad to say, his popularity with the hip-hop crowd has actually increased."

Unsure where the conversation was going, Bertie nodded her head slowly.

"Everyone makes mistakes," the alderman continued, "But not everyone is given a second chance to repair the damage. I'm a generous man, Professor Bigelow. I'd like to offer LaShawn Thomas an opportunity to redeem himself."

Chancellor Grant frowned. "You know my position on this, Fred. LaShawn Thomas is *persona non grata* on this campus."

The alderman's smile remained in place as he set his coffee cup deliberately on the end table next to him.

"Surely you can bend the rules a little. I'd hate to see your funding cut when the finance committee reviews Metro's budget next year."

As Bertie watched silently, Dr. Grant coughed and shifted in his seat.

"Your point is well taken," the chancellor intoned gravely. "However, I have the safety of the entire Metro community to consider. I cannot have dangerous criminals waltzing around the premises."

"Nobody's talking about bringing LaShawn on campus," Steady Freddy said, laughing. "My rally is going to be at the Masonic Lodge on Western Avenue."

"I see." Dr. Grant paused and looked out the window. "I suppose there's no harm in him performing alone, without the choir."

"As long as he's up on stage, I'm happy," the alderman said, smiling more broadly than ever. "In fact, I thought we could sing a little duet together. 'Just the Two of Us' would be appropriate, don't you think?"

"I believe we have reached a consensus," Dr. Grant said. He shifted his gaze to Bertie. "Does this arrangement work for you, Professor Bigelow?"

"Of course," Bertie said. Anything that would burnish LaShawn's image in Dr. Grant's eyes was bound to be a plus. If she could get the boy to act responsibly at the rally, it would also help her in case she ended up appearing before the disciplinary committee. "LaShawn will be singing at the rally if I have to drive him there myself."

The alderman beamed. "I knew you'd understand my position, Professor. May I ask you another small favor?"

"Certainly," Bertie said.

"I was hoping you could give me a few singing lessons. I wouldn't need much, you understand. I was the tenor soloist in my college glee club." The alderman puffed out his chest and bellowed "My Country 'Tis of Thee" in a grating monotone. "As you can see, I've got a pretty good voice. It just needs a little touching-up before LaShawn and I appear onstage together."

"Metro College is at your disposal," Dr. Grant interjected smoothly, ignoring the panicked expression on Bertie's face. "I'm sure the professor will be delighted to help you."

"Here's my card," Bertie added with a weak smile. "Call me any time."

As she left the meeting, Bertie had to bite her lip to keep from laughing. *You have to hand it to Steady Freddy. He's got more tricks up his sleeve than Houdini.* Once LaShawn sang a duet with Steady Freddy onstage, everyone would assume the two had become the best of friends. Of course they weren't—and probably never would be—but in the shadowy world of politics, appearance was far more important than reality. The real question was whether Bertie would be able to convince LaShawn to perform at all, given his grudge against the Alderman.

Back in her office, she dug through her files until she found LaShawn's contact information. The only number he'd listed was that of his grandmother. When Mrs. Petty did not answer her phone, she remembered that LaShawn had said his grandmother worked two jobs and attended church six nights a week. Over the next two days, Bertie tried Mrs. Petty's number several times. But the woman never picked up her phone, nor did she seem to have an answering machine.

By Wednesday afternoon, Bertie was completely frustrated. Despite several more attempts, she had been not been able to reach Mrs. Petty. What was worse, Alderman Clark had left her two messages checking to see if she'd spoken to LaShawn. Worse still, the tryouts for the spring musical had been terrible. Without LaShawn to bolster the cast, it was likely the show would be a flop. The madrigal singers were also floundering. For the third time in as many weeks, her piano students came to class unprepared. When the lead soprano failed to show up for concert choir, Bertie was at her wit's end. Though she was only three weeks into her semester, she felt exhausted, out of sorts, and desperate for musical inspiration.

When the alderman called for a third time that evening, Bertie promised she would have an answer by the weekend, even if she had to camp on Mrs. Petty's doorstep.

"I like your attitude, Professor," Steady Freddy said. "I have an appointment near Metro College in the afternoon tomorrow. How about giving me that singing lesson you promised?"

"Of course," Bertie said, cringing inwardly. From the little snippet of singing he'd treated her to in Dr. Grant's office, the alderman was less musical than a sack of bricks. On the other hand, if giving him vocal coaching would improve her standing with Dr. Grant, she was glad to do it. "My last class finishes at six. I'll wait for you in the music room."

Chapter Seventeen

As usual in Chicago at this time of year, it was bitter cold. As Bertie finished up for the day, sheets of snow angled down from the sky, piling up in ominous drifts on the street outside her classroom window. Students scurried to their cars with lowered heads to avoid the slap of the wind howling down Halsted Street. In weather like this, it seemed unlikely that Steady Freddy Clark would actually show up for his first—and hopefully only—singing lesson.

But sure enough, at six o'clock on the dot, the alderman, dressed in a five hundred dollar cashmere overcoat and broadbrim leather hat, strolled into the music room. In his hand was a battered copy of the sheet music for "Just the Two of Us."

"Now, I want you to treat me the same way you'd treat any other student," he said. He took off his coat and hat and positioned himself in front of the piano. "As I told you, I was quite a singer back in college. But it's been a while."

Bertie nodded. She took a seat behind the piano and ran her fingers over the keys.

"Let's get your voice warmed up, shall we?" She struck a C major chord and began to lead him through a series of simple three-note scales. By the time she'd finished the first exercise, Bertie had confirmed her worst suspicions. Steady Freddy Clark might be a smooth politician and a brilliant tactician, but where music was concerned, the man was dumb as a post. No matter what note she played on the piano, Steady Freddy produced the same tuneless monotone.

"How'd I do?" His face glowed with the joy of singing. "Not too bad for an old guy, if I do say so myself."

"You certainly have a strong voice, Alderman Clark," Bertie said.

"Call me Freddy, please. I've always prided myself on the strength of my vocal power. It's a bit of a requirement in my business, you know."

"Yes, well. Tell you the truth, I hardly know where to begin," Bertie said. Which was true. The man was a walking compendium of vocal problems—a singing teacher's worst nightmare.

"In that case, let's begin with my song," Steady Freddy said. "As you know, I intend to sing this with LaShawn Thomas at my campaign rally next week. Show of unity and all. Speaking of which, have you spoken to the young man recently?"

"Not yet," Bertie said. As she saw the alderman's face darken, she added hastily, "I'm sure he'll be delighted to perform with you. If I'm not mistaken, he sang 'Just the Two of Us' for the spring concert last year." Bertie had read somewhere that big lies were often more believable than small ones. If Bertie had been Pinocchio, her nose would have grown a foot behind the whopper she'd just told.

"Really? In that case, I'd better step up my game." Steady Freddy laughed. "Wouldn't want to embarrass myself in front of my public."

For the next half hour, the Alderman bleated like an ailing billy goat as Bertie accompanied him on the piano. From time to time, she interjected what she hoped were tactful suggestions to help him remain on pitch. These comments Freddy brushed aside impatiently, insisting that his college choir director had given him all the technical instruction he would ever need.

"I'm just rusty," he insisted. "Let me do it again. This time I'll add more *feeling*." With his chest puffed out and his feet planted wide, he raised his arms and brayed with vigor, "Just the two of us. Ooh yeah! Sock it to me, baby! Talkin' 'bout the two of us."

Keeping her head down, Bertie applied herself to the piano. As long as she didn't look up, there was hope that she could avoid bursting out in laughter.

After three more run-throughs, each more off-key than the last, Steady Freddy glanced at his Rolex.

"Seven o'clock already. My goodness, where has the time gone?"

Bertie could have given him a very precise answer to that question, but she restrained herself. If Steady Freddy was happy, Dr. Grant would be happy. And if Dr. Grant was happy, perhaps she would still have a job when the disciplinary committee met to discuss her case. As the alderman collected his sheet music and put on his coat, she said, "Glad you could stop by today, Alderman Clark. I don't think you'll be needing any more lessons before the rally next week, though. I think your voice has reached its full potential."

"When ya got it, ya got it." Steady Freddy's face glowed with pride. "Told you I was the soloist with my college glee club."

"That must have been some choir," Bertie said drily. Fortunately for her, the alderman had absolutely no sense of irony.

"Gotta run," he said. "I'm meeting Momolu Taylor at the Princeton Natural Health Clinic in twenty minutes." He picked up his cashmere coat from its resting place on the chair in front of him and brushed it down carefully. "The man has worked wonders in this community. That Upward Rise Program he's created is outstanding. Not many men would be willing to invest so much time and effort to help our troubled youth the way he does. I'm thinking about nominating him for the Englewood Neighborhood Hero award this year."

Bertie nodded. It was on the tip of her tongue to ask the Alderman whether Dr. Taylor's testosterone supplement was also "working wonders." Instead, she smiled blandly and said nothing.

"Shame about Judge Green passing like that," the alderman said. "Humbert tells me the two of you were close?"

"Not really," Bertie said. When she didn't elaborate, Steady Freddy continued.

"That old buzzard was quite a character. Used to get the strangest notions into his head, always dreaming up one conspiracy theory or another. He even accused me of drug running. Can you imagine?"

"Funny you should say that," Bertie said. "Seems to me LaShawn said something similar at the Christmas concert."

If she'd thought she would be able to unsettle Steady Freddy Clark, Bertie had been seriously mistaken. Without missing a beat, the Alderman burst out laughing.

"So he did, Professor. So he did. Got a great imagination, that boy." He put on his coat and positioned his leather hat at a jaunty angle on his head. "Be sure you speak to LaShawn, Professor Bigelow. He's out on bond now, enjoying his freedom, but Judge Drayton is a close personal friend." Taking hold of Bertie's arm, his jovial expression vanished in an instant. "I'd hate to see LaShawn's bond revoked, wouldn't you? Cook County Jail is no place for a sensitive young man like that."

Without another word, Alderman Steady Freddy Clark turned on his heel and walked out.

Later that night, Bertie's imitation of Steady Freddy singing "Just the Two of Us" had Ellen in stitches. As Bertie sat on her living room couch with a glass of Merlot in one hand and the telephone in the other, she pictured Ellen on the other end of the phone line, reclining in a similar fashion.

"Girl, I have never heard such God-awful singing in my entire life," Bertie said.

"Didn't you say anything?"

"I tried, Ellen. Really I did. But the man is absolutely impervious to criticism. I don't think he heard a single word I said."

"The secret of his political success, no doubt," Ellen said, laughing.

"He was on his way to meet Momolu Taylor at the clinic," Bertie said. "Do you think he was going there to pick up some more Testemaxx?"

"You know how men are. If Dr. Taylor's dick stiffener is as good as advertised, I am sure our beloved alderman is stuffing his briefcase with it as we speak."

"LaShawn said as much at the Christmas concert," Bertie said. "When I tried to ask Freddy about it, he laughed."

"What did you expect? The man's a politician, Bert. Smooth as bacon grease and twice as slippery."

"Still, I think LaShawn was on to something. The alderman let his guard down for a split second just before he left, hinting he had the power to get LaShawn's bond revoked. He acts all friendly and whatnot, but I'll bet he's furious inside."

"Quite naturally. If the little flake had called you a junkie in front of several hundred people, you'd be furious, too."

"When I went by LaShawn's house last week, someone had already been by there looking for him."

"And you think that someone was our beloved Alderman Clark?"

"Could have been," Bertie said thoughtfully. "Some guy in a fancy coat, according to the little kid I talked to. Lord knows the Alderman fits into that category. Whoever it was, LaShawn snuck out of the house to avoid seeing him. I'm beginning to wonder if I did the right thing, getting Mac to bail him out."

"Are you kidding me? Of course you did the right thing. Everybody knows that lockup's a hellhole."

"Then why hasn't LaShawn called me? I've left him a million messages."

"That grandmother of his probably has him in church twenty-four-seven."

"I suppose," Bertie said slowly, "but I'll feel a lot better when the kid turns up, that's all."

Ellen laughed. "Speaking of people turning up. Do you remember me talking about Raquib?"

"Your old boyfriend from college? Of course I remember," Bertie said.

"He called me out of the blue last night. I just about fell over when I heard his voice. His ears must have been burning from us talking about him so bad the other day. He just moved to Chicago a couple months ago." In response to Bertie's unspoken question, Ellen said, "And yes. He's single again."

"No more wives? You sure?"

"I'm sure," Ellen said. "We talked on the phone for hours last night." Her voice turned soft and dreamy. "He called again this morning to say he missed me. Isn't that sweet?"

"Sounds obsessive to me," Bertie said. "But yes. It's sweet."

Ellen sighed. "I think I'm in love, Bert."

"What about Jerome? The two of you looked pretty into each other at The Loft Saturday night."

"Oh, Jerome's okay in his way," Ellen said. "But when Raquib and I were together? Girl, it's like we were *made* for each other."

"Long as he's not made for five other women at the same time," Bertie said.

"Trust me. The brother has really straightened up his act. He prays five times a day. Doesn't smoke. Doesn't drink. All that clean living clears a man's head, Bert."

"Not to mention what it does for his stamina."

"Shut up," Ellen said, giggling. "You're making me blush."

Bertie felt a pang of envy as she hung up the phone. She and Delroy had been happily married for more than ten years—so much in harmony they'd finished each other's sentences. But in the nine months since Delroy's death, Bertie could not deny she was beginning to miss having a man in her life. If she'd been a more carefree type of person, Bertie would already have begun to date. But Bertie was not a carefree type of person. Not when it came to men, anyway. If she were going to be with someone again, it would have to be true love, the way it had been between her and Delroy. As she stared listlessly out her living room window, Bertie felt a single tear trickle down her cheek. In her heart of hearts, she knew she'd never find that kind of happiness again. Not now. Not ever.

Impulsively, she picked up the phone and dug out her credit card. Ten minutes later, Bertie Bigelow was the proud owner of a front row ticket to the following night's performance of *Porgy and Bess* at the Lyric Opera. The cost of the ticket was scandalous—nearly a week's pay—but it would be worth it to see the amazing Audra McDonald perform. Bertie might never again experience true love, but for the moment, she still had a job. And what was the use of having a job if you couldn't treat yourself to a show from time to time?

Chapter Eighteen

In the faculty lounge the next morning, Bertie treated her surprised colleagues to an impromptu rendition of "I've Got Plenty of Nothin'," embellishing her voice with a few choice dance steps. Not to be outdone, Maria Francione jumped off the battered couch in the corner and joined Bertie in jitterbugging around the room.

"The student activities center is down the hall," Jack Ivers groused, ostentatiously moving his chair into a corner out of harm's way. "This place is supposed to be for grown-ups. What in the world has gotten into you, Bertie?"

"I'm seeing *Porgy and Bess* at the Opera House tonight," Bertie said, her face radiant with excitement.

"*Porgy* is one of my favorite shows," Francione chimed in. "There's more bad behavior on display than your average Jerry Springer episode. You've got pimps and drug addicts, gambling and knife fights, a murder, a noble cripple, and a young girl headed for trouble. What more could anyone want?"

For the rest of the day, Bertie whistled Gershwin tunes as she walked around campus. The minute she got home from work, she intended to soak herself in a scented bubble bath and spend the next two hours dressing up. A black Jovani gown with a lace top hung in readiness at the front of her closet, along with the mink stole Delroy had given her for her birthday.

But as Bertie approached her office at the end of the day, Bree Harris and a delegation of students from the music theater club were waiting for her.

"We thought you'd never get here," Harris said peevishly. With her bronze complexion, high cheekbones, and elegant diction, the girl was a dead ringer for Diana Ross. The only thing Bree Harris lacked was talent. However, the fact that she could not carry a tune in a bucket hadn't stopped the girl from electing herself the *de facto* authority regarding all things musical on campus.

"How nice to see you, Bree," Bertie said, pasting a smile on her face. In as cheerful a voice as she could muster, Bertie invited the students in. For the next forty-five minutes, she listened to their complaints about the future of the new Music Theater Society. Apparently, two competing factions were vying for the presidency. In the middle of what was becoming a very heated conversation, Bertie's extension rang.

"Mrs. B? It's me, LaShawn."

Bertie's relief at hearing from the boy was quickly overcome by irritation.

"Where on earth have you been, LaShawn? I've been calling your grandmother all week trying to find you."

LaShawn did not reply. Putting her hand over the receiver, Bertie gestured for Brie and her friends to continue their discussion without her.

"LaShawn? Are you still there?"

"Yeah, I'm here."

"Listen," Bertie said. "I need you to perform in a special concert next week."

Instead of being excited or even curious, the boy was silent. After a long pause, he said, "I've had a couple things come up, Mrs. B. Can we talk?"

"I'm in the middle of a meeting right now." Bertie stole a glance at her watch. "Can you call back in an hour?"

"That'll be too late," LaShawn mumbled softly. "Never mind. I'll give you a call Monday."

"Make sure you do, LaShawn. You and I have got to talk. Nine a.m. sharp, okay?"

"Yeah, sure, Mrs. B. No problem." LaShawn's voice was definitely softer than usual. "Can you give me Miss Petrowski's extension? I need to ask her something."

Cradling the phone on her shoulder, Bertie pulled a battered copy of the Metro College directory from her desk drawer.

"She's probably already gone for the weekend, but you can leave her a message. Her extension is 2363. Call me Monday morning, LaShawn. Don't forget."

It was nearly six thirty by the time Bree Harris and her friends left Bertie's office. There was no time to change or even to eat dinner, but if she hurried, Bertie might make it to the Opera House on time. Fortunately, traffic on the Dan Ryan Expressway was relatively light, and she was able to find a parking spot along Wacker Drive. Out of breath and severely underdressed for the occasion, Bertie slid into her seat just as the house lights went down. But as soon as the conductor stepped onto the podium, her troubles slipped away. The sets, costumes, and orchestra were first-rate, the supporting cast terrific, and Audra McDonald was every bit as fabulous as Bertie had hoped.

Somewhere in the middle of Act One, Bertie's growling stomach reminded her that she had not eaten since breakfast that morning. Normally, her inner economist flinched at spending $15 for a tuna melt, but tonight she felt like treating herself. Leaving just as the curtain came down for intermission, Bertie walked briskly to the mezzanine level, snagging one of the last available tables in the elegantly decorated snack bar.

As Bertie took her seat, a tiny, sparrow-like woman waved to her from the end of the long line of people waiting to get into the restaurant.

"Yoo hoo, Bertie! It's me, Mabel Howard. Mind if I join you?"

Without waiting for an answer, the Hot Sauce King's wife scooted under the velvet rope that marked off the entrance to the dining area and plopped herself down at Bertie's table.

"Phew," she said, daubing her brow with an elegant lace handkerchief. "A body could die from hunger waiting in that line out there. Who'd have thought so many folks would want to eat a fifteen dollar sandwich in the middle of the night." Like her husband, Mabel Howard hailed from a small town in rural Georgia. Unlike her husband, Mabel Howard was a chatterbox who wore her heart guilelessly on her sleeve. "For the kind of money they're charging, they oughta be throwing down with some ribs in this joint."

"I doubt if it would go over with the clientele," Bertie said with a smile. "Do you come here often?"

Mabel Howard leaned in closer. "This is my very first time," she whispered. "I'm tryin' to look like I fit in. How'm I doin' so far?"

Bertie made an "o" with her thumb and forefinger for the okay sign.

"Perfect, Mabel. I'd have never guessed. That's a fabulous gown you're wearing? Is it a Versace?"

"Actually, it's a copy, but don't tell my husband. He gave it to me for my birthday last year. Paid a fortune for the damn thing. I didn't have the heart to tell him he'd been overcharged."

"Well, copy or no, it's dazzling. That red velvet brings out the highlights in your hair."

"Thanks, Bertie. My husband, bless his heart, never notices a thing I wear. He knows I like to dress up, so he buys me things. But he'd probably be just as happy to see me in overalls and a dirty T-shirt."

"So how is Mr. Howard? Is he here with you tonight?" Ever since her run-in with the Hot Sauce King the week before, Bertie had dreaded the inevitable occasion when their paths would cross.

"He was supposed to come," Mabel said, shaking her head. "Would you believe it's our anniversary tonight? Charley promised he'd take me some place grand to celebrate. We bought these tickets months ago, but at the last minute something came up. Business, he said. I pitched a fit, of course, but he wouldn't budge."

Bertie smiled sympathetically. "I imagine your husband's new restaurant must be keeping him pretty busy."

"Long as it's the restaurant and not some gold-digging young heifer, I sp'ose it's okay," Mabel said, twirling her fork thoughtfully. After a pause, she brightened. "Charley interviewed one of your students for a job yesterday. A tall, skinny kid with his hair in cornrows."

"LaShawn Thomas?" Bertie raised her eyebrows in surprise. "I didn't know he was interested in restaurant work."

"Yep, that's the one. When Charley described the kid to me, I remembered we'd already met him. In an elevator at the Jackson Towers, of all the ridiculous places."

Bertie lost all interest in her tuna sandwich. "How unusual," she said in what she hoped was a light conversational tone. "How long ago was this?"

"We met on New Year's Eve. Isn't that wild? While Charley and I were in the elevator on our way down from Mrs. Leflore's penthouse, my husband decided to drop in on Judge Green." Mabel frowned. "Can I tell you something in confidence? I know it's not right to speak ill of the dead, but the judge was a very unpleasant man, always looking for the worst in people. When Charley said he wanted to visit the judge, I said I'd take the elevator on down and wait in the lobby. And *that* is where I met your student, Bertie."

"In the elevator?"

"Well, sort of. When the elevator opened on the judge's floor, Charley got off and LaShawn got on. Do you know he sang me a song? Right there in the elevator. What a beautiful voice. I swear to God, he sounds just like Usher. Absolutely amazing. It was definitely meant to be that he showed up at the Hot Link Emporium looking for a job. Do you follow the stars, Bertie? I do. 'Course I'm a Pisces, which is a water sign. That naturally makes me a dreamer."

Normally, Mabel's aimless prattle would have irritated Bertie. But at the moment, she was grateful for the woman's nonstop monologue. It gave her time to think. Charley Howard had said he was in Mrs. Leflore's penthouse when the judge was shot. Apparently, he'd lied. More intriguing still, LaShawn had seen the Hot Sauce King get out of the elevator on the judge's floor the night of the murder. As Mabel blathered on about her rising sign and its effect on her moon sign, Bertie pondered her next move. Whatever she said, she must not let Mabel realize she was destroying her husband's alibi for the murder of Theophilus Green.

"I don't know a lot about astrology, but isn't the time of day an important factor?" Bertie said. "You don't happen to remember what time it was when you saw LaShawn do you? His stars and your stars must have been in alignment at the exact same moment." Mabel responded to the question without a hint of suspicion, just as Bertie had hoped.

"Gee, you know, you're right," Mabel said. "I'll have Sister Destina do a reading when I see her next week. It could be very important. Fortunately, I know exactly what time it was when I met the boy. It was one fifty-two a.m. precisely."

"How on earth can you possibly be so exact?"

"When we were leaving Mrs. Leflore's apartment, Charley and I got into this big argument about whether it was 2013 on the West Coast yet. Our daughter lives in California, and I wanted to wish her a Happy New Year. He kept saying they were three hours behind. I knew it was only two, and I was right. I made him look it up on his phone before we got on the elevator."

Bertie nodded absently. As Mabel chattered on, it was obvious she had no idea the police considered LaShawn a suspect in Judge Green's murder. Apparently, Mabel was more interested in the activities of the stars than she was in the activities of her fellow humans. Charley Howard was not likely to have been so oblivious. What had he and

LaShawn talked about yesterday? Was it really a job interview, or had it been something more?

When the bell announcing the end of intermission rang, Bertie paid the tab.

"Just think of it as an anniversary gift," she said, giving Mabel Howard a hug and a peck on the cheek.

All through the second half of the performance, Bertie found it hard to concentrate on the action unfolding onstage. If Charley Howard had seen the judge that night, he would be able to give LaShawn an alibi for the murder. Of course, if Howard had visited the judge after LaShawn left, he could very well be the murderer himself.

Chapter Nineteen

It was nearly midnight by the time Bertie returned home. She changed into her nightgown and wandered into the kitchen to fix herself a late-night cup of cocoa. After pouring some milk and a generous spoonful of cocoa powder into the pan to heat, Bertie sat down at the kitchen table to think. Should she confront LaShawn about his visit to the Hot Sauce King when she talked to him Monday morning? Or should she play her cards closer to her chest and see what explanation LaShawn provided for his behavior?

Should she tell David Mackenzie? He was a close friend and a former prosecutor. Surely he could help her decide what to do. But it was nearly one a.m. What if his wife were to answer the phone? The two women had not spoken since Angelique's meltdown at the dinner party two weeks ago. Much as Bertie would like to talk things over with Mac, it would have to wait for a more appropriate time.

Policemen, on the other hand, were on call twenty-four-seven. Should she call Detective Kulicki and tell him what she'd found out? Once Bertie brought the police into it, the wheels of justice would begin to grind inexorably forward. But what if she were wrong? Like many African Americans, Bertie tended to view the police with suspicion. In her experience, they tended to shoot first and ask questions later, especially where black men were concerned.

Maybe Ellen Simpson would be able to suggest the best course of action. After all, she was a brilliant woman and a committed social activist. Laboriously, Bertie tapped out a message on her cell phone.

You still up? It's Bertie. I need some advice.

Ellen's reply came seconds later: *Call me tomorrow, okay? Raquib is here & I'm in love!*

Feeling frustrated and more than a little sorry for herself, Bertie extracted a bottle of cognac from the cupboard and added a stiff dose to her cup. Tomorrow, at a respectable hour, she'd give Mac a call. Later still, she'd check in with Ellen. Until then, she was going to put LaShawn, the Hot Sauce King, and Theophilous Green's murder completely out of her mind.

At four forty-five, Bertie's cell phone startled her awake. Trapped inside the device's miniature speaker, her Marvin Gaye ringtone played "What's Goin' On?" over and over. The phone should have been right beside her bed, but, of course, it wasn't. After a brief pause, Marvin began to sing again.

By the time Bertie finally located her phone, it had stopped ringing. She staggered into the bathroom and splashed some cold water onto her face. *Most likely some drunk who couldn't see straight enough to punch in the right digits. No friend of mine would dare call me at this hour.* Bertie was just tucking the blankets back around her neck when Marvin began to sing again. Heaving a reluctant sigh, she rolled out of bed and picked up the phone.

"I should *never* have trusted you!" LaShawn's grandmother was screaming. "You lied to me. You and that fancy lawyer friend of yours."

In as calm a tone as she could muster, Bertie replied, "What is it, Mrs. Petty? Has something happened to LaShawn?"

"My baby's dead, Mrs. Bigelow. You promised to help. Instead, you got him killed."

Bertie's stomach ached as though it had been kicked. As Mrs. Petty continued to harangue her, alternating between screaming and weeping, Bertie stared numbly around the room. LaShawn? Dead?

How could that be? She'd just talked to him the day before. He'd promised to call first thing Monday morning. Surely there'd been some kind of mistake. When Mrs. Petty finally calmed down enough to be coherent, Bertie realized that there had been no mistake. LaShawn Thomas was dead—killed in a drive-by shooting in Englewood the night before.

"What did the police say?" Bertie asked her. "Has anyone been arrested?"

"When someone gets killed in your neighborhood, the cops make arrests," Mrs. Petty said bitterly. "Around here, no one cares."

Bertie lived in an integrated, middle-class neighborhood near the University of Chicago. Though she didn't think of herself as privileged, the brutal truth was she and Lurlean Petty inhabited vastly different worlds.

"I'm so terribly sorry," Bertie mumbled. Even as she said them, her words felt weak and futile. "I only wanted to help the boy, Mrs. Petty. You've got to believe me."

Now that she'd vented her anger and grief, Mrs. Petty began crying softly.

"LaShawn was my heart, the light of my life. I practically raised him after his mama got the AIDS. When his father was killed, I did everything I could to keep LaShawn safe. But for whatever reason, the good Lord has decided to call my baby home. Sherelle and her son, Benny, are all the family I got left."

For a moment, both women were silent.

"As God is my witness, I will do what I can to find out what happened to your grandson," Bertie said, wiping away a tear with the back of her hand.

"You do that," Lurlean Petty said and hung up.

When David Mackenzie phoned later that morning, his mood was somber.

"Detective Kulicki filled me in on the details earlier today," Mac told her. "As murders go, LaShawn's was pretty routine. Sometime

120

between midnight and two a.m., a black SUV approached LaShawn as he stood at the corner of 63rd and Stewart. Shots were fired. When the car drove away, LaShawn was dead. Several people saw the SUV and heard the shots. But beyond that, no one's talking. No one will admit to having seen the license plate or any other distinguishing characteristics about the car. The kid was just in the wrong place at the wrong time, Bertie. This case might never be solved."

Chapter Twenty

Metro Community College went into mourning as news of LaShawn's death spread among students and faculty. In the halls between classes, fearful students gathered in clusters to grieve. Instead of the usual routine at choir practice, Bertie used the time to let students share their feelings about death, about LaShawn, and about the growing violence on the streets of the city. As the day progressed, Bertie found herself becoming angrier and angrier. This was America, not Baghdad. There was something deeply wrong with a society in which a bright, talented, and unarmed young man could be brazenly gunned down in the middle of the street. No arrests had been made, and as far as Bertie knew, the police were not even questioning possible suspects.

At lunchtime, there was none of the usual banter in the faculty lounge. Red-eyed from weeping, Maria Francione sobbed dramatically in the corner. At the opposite end of the room, Jack Ivers brooded in stoic silence. As Bertie refilled her mug from the office coffee machine, Letitia Petrowski caught her eye.

"I want you to know how sorry I am about those terrible things I said the other day," she said. "LaShawn was my student, too, you know. It's true I got frustrated with him at times, but only because I saw how bright he was."

When Bertie nodded absently, the science teacher continued. "I may have been the last person on earth to speak with him before he was shot. Isn't that strange? LaShawn called me Friday night. He wanted to know if I knew what isopropyl nitrite was. Said he'd found a case of the stuff and wanted to know if it was legal."

Slowly, Bertie put down her coffee cup. "And is it? Legal, I mean."

"Depends what you're using it for," Petrowski said. "It's an inhalant reputed to have aphrodisiac properties. If you sell it to others for that purpose, it's illegal. But if you're selling it as a 'room deodorizer,' it's perfectly legal. When I asked why he wanted to know, LaShawn said it was for an extra credit project he was doing to make up for all the classes he'd missed. He said his suspension was about to be lifted and that he'd show me the drug on Monday." She daubed the corners of her eyes with a napkin. "Isn't that something?"

It certainly was. Letitia Petrowski had no idea just how much of a something. Bertie hurried out of the lounge and called David Mackenzie.

"Mackenzie, Broward, and Jones," his receptionist answered. As Bertie waited impatiently for Mac to pick up his extension, it crossed her mind that it would probably have been better to send an email. But it was too late for that now. Several minutes ticked by before Mac finally came to the phone.

"I'm in the middle of an important meeting right now," he said irritably. "Can I call you later?"

"This will only take a second, I promise." Her news was too important to wait. "The night he was killed, LaShawn told his chemistry teacher he had a case of isopropyl nitrite. It's illegal to sell the stuff except as a room deodorizer. He was going to bring it to show her on Monday."

David Mackenzie sighed. "Stay out of this, Bertie. Meddling in a murder case like this could be dangerous. LaShawn's death is a police matter now."

"But don't you see?" Bertie persisted. "I think he got the stuff from the Princeton Avenue Natural Health Clinic. The place is only two blocks from where he was killed."

"It doesn't matter what you think," he snapped. "A murder investigation is no place for amateurs."

Stung, Bertie did not respond.

"Give it a rest," Mackenzie said in a gentler tone. "Let the police handle it." Without waiting for her reply, the lawyer hung up.

Bertie felt like kicking herself. *What an idiot you are, bothering the man at work like that.* Mac had said to call him anytime, but obviously he hadn't meant it literally. Clearly she'd been paying more attention to Ellen's intuitions than they deserved. David Mackenzie was most definitely not "sweet" on her. At this moment, Bertie suspected the man didn't like her at all. *He probably thinks I'm a hopeless, hysterical spinster*, she thought bitterly. *The way I've been behaving lately, he's probably right.*

Chagrined, Bertie dug through her purse, extracted Detective Kulicki's card, and punched in his number. When her call went straight to voice mail, Bertie left a brief message telling him about the isopropyl nitrite LaShawn may have taken from the Princeton Natural Health Clinic.

After leaving a second message on Kulicki's answering machine when she got home from work that evening, Bertie poured herself a cup of tea and sat down at her kitchen table to brood. In theory, Mac was right. The job of solving murders should be left to trained professionals. But on the South Side of Chicago, the police were outmanned and outgunned. In the Englewood neighborhood alone, there had been three gang-related shootings in the two days since LaShawn's death. With a war like that on his hands, she doubted Detective Kulicki would be getting back to her any time soon.

To bring LaShawn's killer to justice, concerned citizens were going to have to get involved. If Big Mac was too busy to help, Bertie was just going to go it alone. As she poured herself another brandy, Bertie imagined what would happen if she were able to solve the crime. As the police led LaShawn's killer—whomever it turned out to be—away in handcuffs, she pictured David Mackenzie on his knees, begging her forgiveness.

"I was wrong," he'd say as tears streamed down his face. "I should have never doubted you, Bertie."

In order to make this satisfying fantasy come true, however, she was going to have to figure out why LaShawn was murdered. Despite the fact that he was killed in a drive-by shooting, LaShawn Thomas was not and had never been a gang member. Of that, Bertie was positive. But if LaShawn had not been killed in some kind of gang war, then why?

Could his murder have had anything to do with the cache of isopropyl nitrite he found? The answer to that depended on where LaShawn had found the drugs. Supposing, for the sake of argument, that he found them at the Princeton Avenue Natural Health Clinic. If the clinic was selling isopropyl nitrite illegally, Dr. Momolu Taylor would have a motive for murder. If Alderman Clark was mixed up in Taylor's Testemaxx racket, he might also have a motive. Either way, the clinic appeared to be the logical place to start asking questions.

Bertie fixed herself a second pot of tea and considered her options. At the Octagon Ball, Taylor had given her the impression he was attracted to her. And at The Loft last Saturday, he'd whispered an invitation in her ear. Perhaps she could get the doctor to lower his guard with the help of a little strategic flirting. Perhaps he'd even be willing to give her a tour of the clinic so she could look around.

All she needed was a suitable pretext for her visit.

Two hours later, while mopping her kitchen floor, Bertie Bigelow got an amazing idea.

Chapter Twenty-One

The Princeton Avenue Natural Health Clinic was located in a one-story, brick building underneath the elevated train tracks at the corner of 63rd and Princeton. Forty years ago, this corner had been the center of a thriving business district. Now, block after block stood vacant. The building and its parking lot were surrounded by a six foot chain-link fence topped with barbed wire, a silent testament to the danger of doing business in this neighborhood.

The receptionist was clad in a white lab coat and sported an intricate braided hairdo. She barely looked up from her computer as Bertie approached. "Dr. Taylor is not in the office today. It's Lincoln's birthday," she said, sliding the glass window separating them closed.

As the self-proclaimed Land of Lincoln, Illinois was one of only nine states that celebrated Lincoln's birthday on February 12. Most Chicago businesses remained open, and it had not occurred to Bertie that Taylor would take the day off.

She hesitated in front of the reception window, trying to hide her disappointment. Dressed for maximum impact in a tight fitting, red turtleneck, black leather pants, and a pair of boots with stiletto heels, Bertie had hoped to catch the doctor by surprise.

"Is Mr. Peters around?" she asked, raising her voice to be heard through the window. Now that she'd taken the trouble to get dressed up and drive there, Bertie was reluctant to go home empty-handed.

The girl frowned and opened her window. "What did you say your name was?"

"Bigelow. Bertie Bigelow. I met Mr. Peters at The Loft last week."

The receptionist raised an eyebrow but said nothing. She slid the window shut, stood, and opened a door that no doubt led into the interior of the clinic, shutting it firmly behind her.

Bertie grabbed a two-month-old copy of *People Magazine* from a rack against the wall and sat down in one of the red, plastic chairs across from the receptionist's window. On the other side of the room, an exhausted mother watched her grimy toddlers roll around on the floor.

"You boys stop that right now, you hear?" She leaned over and swatted the boy closest to her. Without missing a beat, the toddler turned and kicked his brother in the knee.

Five minutes later, the receptionist reappeared and waved in Bertie's direction. She turned and walked briskly down a narrow hallway without waiting to see whether Bertie was following her. Though the building looked squat and ugly from the outside, the interior was deceptively large. Bertie counted at least ten separate treatment rooms. At the end of the hallway, her guide turned left into a corridor that ended in three closed doors. Motioning for Bertie to wait, she tapped lightly on the first door before opening it, ushering Bertie into a surprisingly spacious room. The dark paneled walls were covered with plaques, awards, and photos of Peters and Taylor shaking hands with prominent African American politicians.

Jawann Peters sat leafing through a stack of papers at a large desk in the center of the room. He wore black slacks and a yellow silk shirt that had been partially unbuttoned to showcase the gold Black Power fist dangling from a chain around his neck. Bertie took a seat on the green leather armchair across from his desk.

"I would like to create a scholarship in LaShawn Thomas's memory," she said. "To raise the necessary funding, the boy's grandmother has authorized me to sell space in the boy's funeral program. The money will be used to help buy laptops for Metro College students interested in becoming doctors. I was hoping your clinic would consider taking out a full-page ad."

Having come to the end of her pitch, Bertie folded her hands in her lap and willed herself to sit still. Last night her scholarship idea had seemed like a clever pretext for getting into the clinic. But as Peters stared at her, silent and unblinking, Bertie was painfully aware that, unlike Dr. Taylor, this man would not be easily swayed.

"LaShawn Thomas was a cold-blooded murderer," Peters said. His gravelly voice grated like a broken fan belt. "I'm amazed Metro College would want to put his name on anything. I'm sorry he's dead, but far as I'm concerned, the little punk got what he deserved." He leaned back in his chair and stared pensively at the ceiling. After a short pause, he said, "On the other hand, Dr. Taylor and I believe in giving back. That's what our Upward Rise Youth Internship Program is all about. LaShawn worked as an intern in our program, as you know. If you'd like to talk to the rest of our interns about your scholarship idea, they're about to start their weekly staff meeting. If they approve the idea, I will recommend we buy an ad—not so much for LaShawn, but to support our community."

"Just one more quick question," Bertie said. "On the night he was killed, LaShawn told his chemistry teacher he'd found a case of isopropyl nitrite. Do you have any idea where he may have gotten it?"

Peters raised an eyebrow. "Are you suggesting it came from here? It would be illegal for us to sell isopropyl nitrite, Bertie. A clinic run by white people might get away with a slap on the wrist for having it. But us? The city would shut us down in a heartbeat."

Peters had a point. After all, it had taken an antidiscrimination suit masterminded by Delroy Bigelow to get the Princeton Avenue Natural Health Clinic licensed in the first place.

"Let me ask you something," Peters said, leaning forward. "Did LaShawn ever actually show you any bottles of this chemical?"

Bertie shook her head.

"That's what I thought," Peters said with a smug smile. "As usual, the boy lied."

"Still," Bertie said, "if you could just check with Dr. Taylor about this, I'd appreciate it."

Peters studied her with narrowed eyes. "Dr. Taylor is a busy man, Mrs. Bigelow. I doubt he has time for this kind of foolishness. Now, if you'll excuse me, I've got work to do." He stood up and looked at his watch. "Miss Richie will take you downstairs to the Upward Rise meeting room."

The receptionist must have been waiting just outside the door. When Peters opened it, she escorted Bertie through a warren of offices and treatment rooms and down a short flight of stairs. At the bottom of the stairs, she opened the door to a large, windowless room. Posters of the rappers 50 Cent, Kanye West, and Lil Wayne decorated the walls. A large boom box in the corner was playing "63rd & Halsted" by 2 Chainz Diss as a dozen teenagers milled around the room. Raising her voice over the thump thump of the music, Miss Richie said, "This is the Upward Rise meeting room." Having accomplished her mission, she retreated, slamming the door behind her.

As Bertie stood awkwardly in the middle of the room, she wished she'd chosen to wear a less revealing outfit. Not only had she failed to win Peters over with her tight sweater and black leather pants, but she was now getting frank stares from the older boys in the room. She had almost decided to leave when a teenager in a maroon tracksuit entered and shut off the boom box.

"This meeting of the Upward Rise crew is now officially in session," he said. Without a word, the teenagers found seats on the battered armchairs and sofas scattered about the room and focused their attention on the young man who was clearly their leader. Squat and thickly muscled, he appeared to be in his late teens.

"Ranaldo!" he snapped at a lanky kid sporting a do-rag and a diamond stud earring. "There's a lady standing. Didn't your mamma teach you no manners?"

If Bertie had spoken this sharply to her students, she would have had a mutiny on her hands. But Ranaldo simply mumbled, "Okay, Tayquan," and stood up. With a grateful smile, Bertie sank into Ranaldo's seat on the couch.

"This lady here is Mrs. Bigelow," Tayquan continued. "She wants to talk about LaShawn."

Bertie looked out at her audience. Dressed in baggy pants and hoodies, twelve boys ranging in age from fourteen to nineteen studied her with hardened eyes.

"LaShawn Thomas was my student," Bertie began. As she spoke, Tayquan remained standing in the front of the room, his arms folded across his chest. "It's true he was accused of murder. But I have chosen to remember LaShawn as a bright and talented young man with a lot to offer this community. It's a crying shame he was taken away from us so young. I would like to start a scholarship at Metro College in LaShawn's name."

Though the teenagers' faces remained impassive, Bertie detected a slight thaw in the atmosphere.

"The money would go to help a student, perhaps even one of you, buy the laptop they'll need to succeed at Metro. Since Upward Rise was such an important part of LaShawn's life, I was hoping you'd be willing to make a contribution."

"We'll talk it over and let Mr. Peters know in the morning," Tayquan said. When Bertie didn't move to leave, Tayquan spoke again. "Upward Rise meetings are private, Mrs. Bigelow. Members only. Mr. Peters will call you tomorrow."

Bertie nodded and picked up her coat and purse. Apparently, Tayquan was throwing her out. Interesting. As Bertie left the room, she heard Tayquan lock the door behind her.

Chapter Twenty-Two

On the way home, Bertie mulled over what she had seen and heard at the clinic. Although she sympathized with Peters on the issue of discrimination, she couldn't help but wonder if he'd played "the race card" to distract her. And what was up with the Upward Rise program? Why hadn't she been allowed to stay for the meeting? What she needed was a fresh perspective. Fortunately, Ellen was home when she called.

"What's up, girl?" Ellen said. "I was just about to call you. Raquib and I are going out to Charley Howard's new Hot Link joint. Would you like to join us?"

When Bertie tried to beg off, citing her recent run-in with the Hot Sauce King, her best friend just laughed.

"Don't be so paranoid, Bertie. The man's probably forgotten all about you by now. We'll pick you up at seven."

When Ellen pulled her car in front of Bertie's house half an hour later, she was alone and wearing a glum expression. In response to Bertie's unspoken question, Ellen said, "Raquib couldn't make it."

"I'm sorry," Bertie said. "Let's just hang out some other time. I don't want to mess up your love life."

"Nonsense," Ellen replied. "Raquib and I have been together exactly one week. In that time, he's refused to meet any of my friends. If I didn't know better, I'd suspect he was up to something."

"Maybe he is," Bertie said. "I know he was the love of your life in college, but let's face it, a person can change a lot in twenty years."

"No way," Ellen said firmly. "I can tell when a man is on the up-and-up. How else could he be so sweet to me?"

Bertie decided the best response to Ellen's last statement was to change the subject for the rest of the drive.

Over steaming platters of soul food, she described her visit to the Princeton Natural Health Clinic. When Bertie was finished, Ellen sat lost in thought for several minutes.

"I'm a little embarrassed to tell you how I know this," Ellen said. "But isopropyl nitrite is a sex drug. Although it's illegal to sell it for that purpose, men take it to get hard. If Taylor's putting isopropyl nitrite in that dick stiffener of his, he'd be putting his whole business at risk. Have you talked to Mackenzie?"

Bertie reddened and looked down at her plate. "Last time we spoke, Mac told me I should give the whole thing a rest. He said it was time to let the police take over."

"Have you talked to the cops then?"

Bertie sighed. "I've called Detective Kulicki a few times, but he hasn't gotten back to me."

"He's probably got his hands full. The way these fools are gangbanging over there, you might not hear from the man for months."

"The clinic has got some kind of youth program going on in the basement. I got to meet some of the kids, and believe me, they were tough. Some of them could definitely be gang members. When I was done speaking, they threw me out of their meeting and locked the door. Do you think they had something to hide? They definitely did not want me hanging around."

"Of course they didn't want you around," Ellen said. "They're *teenagers*. When I was fifteen, I was positively allergic to adults."

An eager young waiter materialized at Bertie's elbow carrying a bottle of wine.

"Is your name Bertie Bigelow? Mr. Howard would like you to accept this bottle of French Champagne with his compliments." As Bertie sat dumbfounded, the boy continued. "Mr. Howard also asked if you would be willing to speak privately with him in his office for a few minutes."

"Mrs. Bigelow would be delighted," Ellen said, her ever-present copper bracelets jangling emphatically. "Please tell the Hot Sauce King not to keep her too long, though. Otherwise, I might be forced to drink this whole bottle by myself."

As Bertie followed the waiter through the swinging doors that led into the kitchen, her thoughts chased each other in frantic circles. Last time she'd talked to Charley Howard, Bertie had practically accused him of murder. *Good thing Ellen's with me,* she thought grimly. *If the Hot Sauce King has a Mafia hit man waiting for me back in his office, she can tell the police who did it.*

Charley Howard's office was at the bottom of a narrow flight of stairs. As offices go, it was considerably less than deluxe. Several cartons of Heavenly Hot Sauce lay piled against the wall on the left. Lining the right-hand wall were shelves containing oversized cans of condiments, industrial kitchen appliances, and sacks of flour. Smack in the middle of all this clutter, the Hot Sauce King sat smoking a cigar with his feet up at a small metal desk piled high with cookbooks.

"Have a seat," he boomed. "Ever since we last met, I've been meaning to apologize for blowing my stack at you the way I did. I'm a big man with a big mouth and a big temper. Can you forgive me?"

"Of course, Charley. I'm sure we'll be running into each other from time to time, what with you becoming an official member of the Octagon Society and all. No need to let bad feelings stand between us."

The Hot Sauce King grinned. "Now that that's settled, I'd like to ask you something. My wife wants to become cultured in the worst way. You know, the symphony, the art museum, high-class stuff like that. Personally, I could care less. I'm way too busy here at the

133

restaurant for that kind of foolishness. Would you consider hanging out with her? I know she likes you, Bertie. What do you say?"

Bertie smiled. In spite of his bluster and violent reputation, Charley Howard apparently had a soft spot.

"Have her give me a call. I'd be delighted to have some company. That reminds me, though. The night I saw her at the opera, Mabel said LaShawn Thomas came to see you last week."

The Hot Sauce King scowled and stubbed out his cigar. "Yeah, that's right. He wanted me to put him in touch with the Roselli mob."

"And did you?"

"Of course not," Howard snapped. "All that stuff is behind me now. I'm a respectable businessman with respectable associates. I'm a goddamn Octagon, for cryin' out loud. The last thing in the world I need is to bring Tony Roselli back into my life. Believe me. I told the kid, in no uncertain terms, to take a hike."

"Did LaShawn say why he wanted to meet Roselli?"

"How should I know? The little snot even tried to blackmail me. He said he'd tell the cops he saw me outside the judge's apartment on New Year's Eve if I didn't do what he wanted." Howard shook his head in disgust. "I just don't know what's wrong with these kids today, Bertie. They got no respect for anybody anymore."

"But you *were* outside the judge's apartment that night. Mabel told me herself."

Charley Howard's feet hit the floor with a bang as he catapulted out of his desk chair.

"I went by to see the judge, I'll admit it. But the man refused to open his door to me, and that's the God's honest truth. I was up there less than five minutes. You can ask my wife."

"Five minutes is more than enough time to shoot someone," Bertie said mildly.

"Out!" Charley Howard shouted. Veins pulsed in his massive neck. "Dammit, I try to be nice. I try to be friends. And what do you give me? Accusations and lies. Out!"

As Bertie scurried up the stairs and out into the restaurant, something told her she'd just had her last drink at Howard's Hot Link Emporium.

"Girl, you must have a death wish," Ellen said as she piloted her Volvo down Stoney Island Avenue. "In the past three weeks, you've accused Charley Howard of murder not once, but twice. Don't you want to live?"

Bertie said nothing. Her teeth were chattering, and not from the cold. What on earth was the matter with her? Ever since she'd become a widow, she seemed unable to behave normally in social situations. Once again, she had allowed her big mouth and boundless curiosity to land her in trouble. If Charley Howard really did kill the judge on New Year's Eve, he could have had his mob friends kill LaShawn when the boy tried to blackmail him. In which case, Bertie was likely to be Howard's next victim. Bertie stared silently out the window as Ellen continued her lecture.

"The minute you walk in your front door, you are going to call Mackenzie. Do you hear me, Bertie? And right after that, you are going to call the cops. *Any* cop." Pulling in front of Bertie's house, Ellen took Bertie by the shoulders and looked her in the eye. "Promise me, okay? Someone out there is killing people. You could be next."

Ellen was right. The idea that Bertie could solve two murders on her own was beyond ridiculous. What's more, it was becoming downright dangerous. Locking her front door carefully behind her, Bertie pulled out her cell phone and punched in Big Mac's number.

"You've reached the Mackenzie residence," his voice sounded tired, even on his answering machine. "We can't come to the phone right now, but please leave us a message. We'd love to hear from you."

Without stopping to take off her coat, Bertie called Detective Kulicki's office, hoping against hope that he would pick up the phone. But, as usual, the policeman was out. After leaving another message on the detective's answering machine, Bertie took off her coat and sat down at the piano. For as long as she could remember, she had consoled herself with music. The night of her husband's funeral, Bertie had gone home, taken the phone off the hook, and played for eight hours straight without stopping. Though her non-musician friends worried that her four-hour-a-day practice habit was becoming a dangerous obsession, her closest friends knew that practicing classical music was Bertie's therapy. She was deep into the second movement of Beethoven's *Moonlight Sonata* when the phone rang.

"I hope I'm not calling too late," Patrice Soule said. Over the phone, the diva sounded like a breathless teenager. "Could you come by my place tomorrow evening? I know it's short notice, but I've got a big show in two weeks. I really need some help getting my music together."

As she got ready for bed that night, Bertie looked forward to doing something she knew she was good at. Tomorrow she would help Patrice Soule learn to read music. While she was at it, perhaps Bertie could give the diva some tips on resolving that mysterious wobble in her voice. And that, Bertie thought as she pulled up the covers, would provide her with all the excitement she would ever need.

Chapter Twenty-Three

"Come in, Bertie. Come in!" Dressed in a skintight pair of purple yoga pants and a Chicago Bulls T-shirt, Patrice Soule hopped from one foot to the other like an eager five year old. "I'm so glad you could come this evening. I know it's late, but it was the only time I had free all day. My Pilates trainer comes in the morning, and then I meet with my manager every afternoon. So thanks, again, for coming. I've had lots of other tutors, but things just never work out. Sometimes I think I'm just too stupid to catch on." The diva giggled nervously. "Sorry, Bertie. I'm babbling again, as usual. Here, let me take your coat."

While Bertie removed her coat and boots, Soule kept up a steady stream of nervous chatter, barely pausing to breathe. Within five minutes, Bertie learned the names of all Soule's previous vocal coaches, the name of her current accompanist, and the fact that the diva was seriously considering replacing him with a thinner man.

"Appearance is everything in this business," she said, hanging Bertie's jacket in a closet by the door. "When I'm up on stage, everything has to be perfect, and that includes my band."

Striding into the living room, she gestured for Bertie to follow. A nine-foot Steinway grand piano, covered with photos of Soule in performance, dominated the room. Holding pride of place among the photographs was an eight by ten color photo of Soule receiving the Illinois Idol trophy from R&B diva Chaka Khan.

"That must have been a proud moment," Bertie said, pointing to the picture.

Soule frowned. "I hate that stupid picture, but Momolu won't let me get rid of it. I look like a blimp in that dress."

"I think you look lovely. Dr. Taylor must be very proud of you."

"Momo is an African aristocrat, you know. He's promised someday he'll take me to sing for Togar Henris, the Liberian millionaire." Soule giggled. "Momo says if Mr. Henries likes my singing, he'll probably give me a present—a gold necklace or maybe one of those sexy Mercedes convertibles to drive."

Bertie smiled. In his manuscript, Delroy had questioned Taylor's claims to royal ancestry. But if Soule wanted to believe her lover was descended from the great Fulani kings of Africa, Bertie was not going to spoil her fantasy. She pulled out the piano bench and sat down.

"Have you done any vocal warmups today?"

"Oh, my God. Should I have done them? I just get so anxious about little things that I forget to do the big things. You know what I mean?" The look of panic in the diva's eyes was unmistakable. "I didn't even offer you a cup of tea. What an idiot I am. Would you like one?"

Without waiting for a reply, Soule bolted into the kitchen, continuing to talk nonstop as she did so.

"Isn't it a shame about LaShawn what's his name getting shot, Bertie?"

Taking a seat on the large, white sofa facing the piano, Bertie agreed that yes, LaShawn's murder was a terrible shame. Today Bertie was determined to stick to the business at hand. She did not intend to take any more diversionary trips into dangerous waters, and she was definitely not going to ask any more nosy questions.

Over the sound of running water and the clatter of pots and pans, Soule continued her rapid-fire monologue.

"Been a lot of people getting themselves killed lately. 'Course, some folks deserve it. Theophilous Green, for instance. He was a *very* bad man." Without waiting for Bertie to reply, Soule rattled on. "The judge had the hots for me, you know. Every time I left the apartment, the crazy old fart would make some excuse to get me alone in the elevator. When Momolu started seeing me, the judge got crazy jealous. He even threatened to go after Momo with *judicial action.*" Soule cackled viciously. "*Judicial action,* my black behind. The only action that Theophilous Green wanted was the action between my legs."

Bertie had promised herself she'd stop letting her curiosity get the better of her. But as Soule continued to chatter on, the temptation to ask a few questions was too strong to resist.

"Is that when you showed the judge your gun?"

"That's right." At last Soule emerged from the kitchen. Two cups of steaming hot tea clattered in their saucers as she set them down on the coffee table. "I'm glad Theophilous is dead. The old bastard had it coming to him. But LaShawn? That's a different story."

"I didn't realize you knew LaShawn," Bertie said. "He was my student, you know. The kid had a wonderful voice."

Soule smiled. "Yeah. He used to sing to me. Usher, of course. Made Momo a little jealous, actually. Whenever I needed to refill my supplements, LaShawn would bring them over from the clinic, special delivery. Now that he's dead, I've got to wait for Momo to bring them." Soule plopped down next to Bertie on the couch. "In fact, I'm waiting for my refill right now. Damn, I wish he'd hurry up."

Bertie took a sip of tea. "What kind of pills are you taking?"

"Weight loss pills, of course. Oops. Forgot the lemon." Soule bounced up off the couch and raced into the kitchen, returning minutes later with a bottle of lemon juice. "Like I told you, I've got a big show coming up. Can't afford to gain a pound."

Bertie surveyed her own generous figure and sighed. Plus-sized divas were commonplace in the world of opera, but pop stars were expected to look like supermodels.

"Do you know what's in the pills?" Bertie said. "There's a lot of stuff out there that's really not healthy."

"You're going to think I'm the dumbest bimbo on the planet, but no. Some kind of African formula Momo prescribed for me." As she spoke, the diva paced nervously around the room, her tea forgotten on the coffee table. "The first week I took them, I lost twenty pounds. I didn't even need to sleep. Girl, I'm telling you, the man's an absolute genius."

Bertie wasn't so sure about that. If the diva walked around this revved up all day, it was no wonder her voice was beginning to fail. The wobble Bertie had detected in Soule's voice would only get worse when coupled with stimulants. If Taylor really cared about this girl, he should have stopped giving her diet pills long ago.

"I don't want to get in your business or anything, but these supplements, whatever they are, are not good for you. They're drying out your vocal cords. If you don't stop soon, you could damage your voice permanently."

Soule stopped dead in her tracks and glared.

"I am the *Illinois Idol*. I don't take orders from anybody. Certainly not from blimpy know-it-alls like you. Who the hell do you think you are?"

The diva's transformation from insecure child to vengeful she-devil was instantaneous. She strode across the room, pulled Bertie's coat from its hanger in the closet, and threw it on the floor.

"Get out!" she screamed at top volume. "This lesson is over. *Now.*"

As Bertie watched in stunned silence, Patrice Soule burst into tears, ran into her bedroom, and slammed the door behind her.

Ellen could not stop laughing when Bertie called to tell her what had happened.

"Girl, they must be putting something funny in the water over there at the Jackson Towers," Ellen said. "Those folks are crazy as bedbugs."

On one level, Bertie's situation was darkly humorous. But viewed from another perspective, it was simply dark.

"All I've done is make people angry," Bertie moaned. "I promised LaShawn's grandmother I'd protect him. I failed. I tried to see if I could turn up any information about the murders. Again, I failed."

"Have you talked to Mac about it?"

"No, and I don't intend to," Bertie said. "I interrupted him in the middle of a meeting the other day." She sighed heavily. "He probably thinks I'm a complete idiot. Or worse still, a lonely widow looking for a knight in shining armor."

"Don't go there, Bertie. You are a strong, capable woman and, if I may say so, still in the prime of life. If you ask me, Big Mac would be more than happy to rescue you any time."

"Just not during a meeting," Bertie said wryly. "If he goes to LaShawn's funeral Monday afternoon, maybe I can talk to him there. Mrs. Petty has asked the choir to sing. Are you going?"

"Wouldn't miss it," Ellen said grimly. "Monday is President's Day. But if Detective Kulicki is worth even half the money the city of Chicago pays him, he'll be there, holiday or no holiday. Be sure you talk to him, Bertie."

As Ellen hung up the phone, Bertie heard a funny sound on the other end of the line, as if someone else were also disconnecting. *Just my luck,* she thought to herself. *On top of everything else, my phone's about to go on the blink.*

Chapter Twenty-Four

Bertie arrived at work the next morning to find a heavyset young woman in her mid-twenties standing outside her office. Dressed in a bulky down parka, jeans, and a pair of no-nonsense Army boots, she leaned against the wall next to Bertie's door with a surly expression on her face.

"You Mrs. Bigelow?"

"That's right," Bertie said. "And you are?"

"Sherelle Davis, LaShawn's sister. Grandma Petty sent me."

Bertie nodded and unlocked her office door. Had Mrs. Petty changed her mind about having the choir sing at the funeral? She had not heard a word from LaShawn's formidable grandmother since the woman's hysterical phone call Saturday morning. Bertie took off her coat, hung it carefully from the hook on the back of her door, and gestured for Sherelle to have a seat. But Sherelle shook her head and remained standing in the center of the room.

"Grandma found this under LaShawn's pillow." She reached into her shoulder bag and extracted a battered spiral notebook. "She's hoping you can figure out what it means. I'm not supposed to leave until you read it."

Bertie took the notebook from Sherelle's outstretched hand. Scrawled across the cover in large capital letters were the words:

REPORT BY AGENT 005 (LASHAWN N. THOMAS)
to CONTROL (JUDGE TG)
TOP SECRET

Bertie turned the page and began to read.

12/28/12 4PM CST—Followed Steady F to the Princeton C and observed him enter. After thirty minutes he left carrying a brown paper bag. I think its Testemaxx in there but don't know for sure. Dr. T walked him out with a big smile on his face. Then I observed Clark cross the street where he engaged in friendly activity (slapping five and hanging out) with 2 suspicious white guys in suits. I never seen them before—bet they're CIA. He handed them the bag, got in his car, and drove away.

Time on the job: 1hr 15mins.—Total fee: $50

Only one more page of the notebook had been filled in. It was dated December 30, the day before Judge Green was killed.

10AM CST—PS leaves bldg. wearing a skintight black jogging suit, fur hat, and mittens. She doesn't see me cause I am standing behind a tree. I follow her to The Bakery at 56th and Cornell Ave. where through the window I observe Dr. T waiting for her. Am not 100% but think he is angry at her. I didn't want to get too close. But he had a mean face on and she was wiping her eyes. I leave before they come out so as not to blow my cover.

Time on the job: 45mins—Total due: $35

When Bertie had finished reading, Sherelle Davis cleared her throat.

"There's no way LaShawn was involved in any gang, Mrs. Bigelow. And I refuse to believe he just got shot by accident. Grandma thinks this notebook could be an important clue," Sherelle said. "What do you think?"

"Looks like Judge Green was paying your brother to follow people around," Bertie said slowly. "The entry dated December thirtieth is about Patrice Soule."

"The Illinois Idol? That woman is a total speed freak," Sherelle said. "LaShawn told me he used to drop a carton of diet pills by her house every couple of days."

"Judge Green was obsessed with her," Bertie said. "He was following her himself, but after she threatened him with a gun, he must have asked LaShawn to do it."

"What about the 'Steady F' in the first entry? Who do you think that is?"

"Alderman Clark, most likely."

Sherelle Davis scowled. "LaShawn ever tell you 'bout the time Steady Freddy called our daddy 'worthless trash' on the six o'clock news? I hope the CIA is involved, Mrs. Bigelow. Maybe they'll waterboard Freddy's sorry ass."

"Sorry to disappoint you," Bertie said drily, "but the whole CIA thing was probably a figment of Judge Green's imagination. The man was a conspiracy nut, I'm afraid."

"Still. Grandma wants you and that fancy lawyer friend of yours to look into it."

"You should take this notebook to the police," Bertie said. "I'm no detective, and neither is Mr. Mackenzie."

"Grandma knows that," Sherelle said impatiently. "That's exactly why she wants you to investigate. The police don't give a rat's ass about LaShawn. He's just another statistic to them. But you were his teacher. You helped my brother when he needed it most."

"I tried to help him," Bertie said. "But let's face it, Sherelle. I failed big time."

"Just think how I feel," Sherelle shot back. "LaShawn would never have got arrested if I hadn't let him keep that stupid gun in my car."

"Why did you let him keep it there? You must have known it was a bad idea. Bad for LaShawn, and bad for you."

"If I'd known it was going to be used to murder somebody, believe me, I'd have put the damn thing in the trash." Sherelle dropped her gaze and bit her lip. "My husband's a soldier in Afghanistan, Mrs. Bigelow. I know all about the harm that guns can do. LaShawn said the gun was a requirement for his job, so I told him to keep it in my car. I didn't want the gun in the house where my seven year old could find it."

"You're Benny's mother?"

"Yeah," Sherelle said, fixing Bertie with a challenging stare. "You got a problem with that?"

"Not at all," Bertie said, smiling. "I met your son a few weeks ago when I came by the house looking for LaShawn. He's a beautiful boy and quite talented. You should think about getting him some music lessons."

"I know Benny loves to sing, Mrs. Bigelow. But right now I'm having a hard enough time making sure he's got food in his belly and a roof over his head." Sherelle Davis sighed heavily. "Don't seem like those music lessons ended up doing LaShawn much good, anyhow."

"Whatever happened to LaShawn had nothing to do with music, Sherelle."

"I suppose. My little brother never could keep his mouth shut. You saw the way he jumped all over Alderman Clark at the Christmas concert. Not that Steady Freddy didn't have it coming, mind you."

"Shortly before he was killed, LaShawn told his chemistry teacher he'd found a crate of isopropyl nitrite."

"Poppers?" Sherelle whistled softly. "No wonder Peters wanted him to carry a gun."

"Any idea who could have stolen it?"

Sherelle Davis shrugged. "In the last six months, three different gangs have moved into the neighborhood. Seems like every day there's something new—a mugging, a robbery, a murder. Now with the Conquering Lions moving in, there's no telling what will happen. I've really got to get going, Mrs. Bigelow. What should I tell my grandmother? You gonna help us or not?"

Bertie sighed. "I never wanted to be a detective, but it looks like I'm turning into one. I'll do what I can, but I can't promise you anything."

For the rest of the morning, Bertie thought about her conversation with Sherelle Davis. With her neighborhood in a state of virtual anarchy, LaShawn's grandmother had lost confidence in the police's ability to solve her grandson's murder. In spite of the fact that Bertie had absolutely no experience as a detective, Mrs. Petty was asking for her help—a sad commentary on life in the Windy City. The least Bertie could do now was to figure out a way to uncover the boy's killer.

Admittedly, she had not had a lot of success recently. Detective Kulicki was not returning her phone calls, and Big Mac had told her, in no uncertain terms, to stay away from the case. Still, the "surveillance reports" in LaShawn's notebook did seem like an important clue. Judge Green had been obsessed with Patrice Soule, a diet pill junkie with a volatile temper and a Smith & Wesson nine millimeter handgun. Could Soule have shot the judge in a fit of drug-induced pique? What exactly was Steady Freddy's relationship to the Princeton Avenue Natural Health Clinic? Who were the two white men in suits he'd been talking to? LaShawn had seen the alderman hand over a brown paper bag. Could it have been a bribe? A drug transaction? As she finished her last class for the morning, Bertie made a mental note to dig a little deeper into Alderman Clark's background. According to Delroy's manuscript, Steady Freddy had been nearly kicked out of college for cheating. It was at least possible Steady Freddy had continued his dishonest ways.

When Bertie walked into the faculty lounge at lunchtime, Maria Francione greeted her with a hug.

"When I passed by your classroom this morning, the stirring tones of your lovely choir transported me to another realm," the drama teacher gushed.

Bertie would have hardly used the word "stirring" to describe the way her students had sounded, but a compliment was, after all, a compliment.

"Glad you enjoyed it," she said. She took her mug down from the peg over the sink and poured herself a cup of stale coffee.

"You were singing 'Swing Low, Sweet Chariot,' were you not?"

"That's right," Bertie said.

Maria patted Bertie on the back. "Bravo, Bertie. The Negro spiritual is a true American art form—a living demonstration of the power of art to transcend the pain of human existence."

"As you could probably tell, we still have a lot of work to do on the arrangement," Bertie said. "But if we do it justice, there will not be a dry eye in the house when we're done."

"Speaking of emotional things, I have a proposition for you." Suddenly bashful, Francione cleared her throat and looked down at the ground. "I've got a script I've been working on. The story of a gutsy Italian girl who moves to Chicago and has a steamy affair with an African American actor. It's my *magnum opus*, you might say."

As Bertie waited politely, Francione paused and took a deep breath before plunging ahead.

"So here's the thing. Since the story has a significant African American aspect to it, I thought it would benefit from some authentic African American music, you follow me? In fact, I'm thinking of adding a revival scene to the work—lots of hallelujahs, amens, and that sort of thing. Do you think your choir would be willing to lend their voices to my dramatic effort? I couldn't pay them, of course. But it would still be an educational experience, don't you think?"

Bertie smiled. "This gutsy Italian girl wouldn't just happen to be you, would it?"

Francione flushed. "Perhaps. But of course, a lot of dramatic license has been taken, Bertie. A *lot*."

"Tell you what. The choir is booked solid for the rest of the semester, but let's talk more about this. Maybe we could put something together for the fall." Bertie picked up her cup and turned away. A pile of Theory 101 papers lay uncorrected on her desk, and she was determined not to let herself get even further behind in her work.

On the other side of the room, Ellen and Jack Ivers were involved in a heated political argument. Dressed in a vibrant-red pantsuit decorated with Ghanaian Adinkra symbols, Ellen had backed the gray-haired professor into a corner and was shaking a finger in his face. When she saw Bertie preparing to leave the room, however, Ellen conceded the argument and walked away, leaving Ivers open-mouthed in her wake.

"Are you going to your office, Bertie?" she said. "I need to get your opinion on something."

After making sure the door to Bertie's office was fully closed, Ellen assumed her customary perch on the edge of Bertie's desk. "For the last three days, I've been getting these spooky vibes. You know, the kind you get when someone stares at you from across a room?"

Bertie nodded.

"Last night, Raquib took me out for Valentine's Day."

"Sounds romantic," Bertie said, hoping she didn't sound too envious. While Ellen and Raquib shared a candlelight supper, she had spent the night alone with her TV and a large bowl of popcorn.

"It was plenty romantic," Ellen said. "But here's the creepy part. We're having fondue at Geja's Café. All of a sudden this black guy sits down alone at the next table. When we get up to leave, he calls for his check. Even though he's only halfway through eating. And I'm almost positive he followed us outside."

"Lots of people leave without finishing their dinner, Ellen. Most likely, he was late for an appointment or something."

"I don't think so, Bert. The man was following us. Now that I think about it, I'm almost positive I saw that same Negro on the street outside my apartment Tuesday night."

"Why on earth would anybody want to follow you?"

Ellen hopped off the desk, opened the door, and peered down the hallway in both directions. Satisfied that the coast was clear, she closed the door and whispered, "Raquib has a history, Bertie. Apparently, he said some things after 9/11 that put him on the FBI's radar."

"Raquib disbanded his cult ten years ago," Bertie said. "You told me so yourself. Most likely the FBI has figured that out by now. You sure you're not just being paranoid?"

"Raquib has been acting real nervous lately. Looking over his shoulder. Crossing in the middle of the street. It's beginning to creep me out."

"Look, Ellen. I don't want to tell you your business, but you've been seeing this guy for less than two weeks. He may have been the love of your life back in the day, but let's face it, people change. Have you thought about backing off a little?"

Ellen sighed. "Of course I have. It's just that when we're alone together, it's just so perfect. When he puts R. Kelly on the stereo, girl, he *moves* me."

Bertie smiled. "Glad to see you have a grip on the really important things in life. But I still think you're being melodramatic. Chances are everything is perfectly fine."

"Hope you're right," Ellen said. She climbed off the desk and smoothed down her pantsuit. "You free tomorrow? I think I need a little shopping therapy. Let's run down to Water Tower Place and buy some new clothes."

Chapter Twenty-Five

SATURDAY, FEBRUARY 16, 2013—NOON

As Bertie took her place in the long line of cars waiting to enter the garage underneath Water Tower Place, Ellen shook her head in exasperation.

"Holy crap, Bertie. What are all these people doing here?"

"Shopping, I expect," Bertie said mildly. "Same as us. It's Saturday afternoon, after all."

Twenty minutes later, after locating a parking spot and walking the equivalent of five city blocks to the mall entrance, the two women stood in front of Armani Exchange, gazing at the new spring fashions. On the salary they made at Metro College, neither woman could afford to shop there, but it was always fun to look. Bertie, who kept a sharp eye out for off-season sales and specials, made a mental note of the items she'd come back for in April. For the next two hours, the women moved in a leisurely manner from store to store, peering in windows and occasionally venturing in to try something on. In the shoe section of Macy's, Ellen sat next to Bertie, leaned over, and whispered, "Don't look now, but he's back."

"Who's back?" Bertie asked. She bent over and yanked an overpriced designer boot off her left foot.

"You know, the man. The man that's been following me."

"In the shoe section of Macy's? I hope his credit card is paid up," Bertie said, laughing.

"Shh," Ellen whispered urgently. "He was behind us in line at The Limited and in the next aisle when we went in The Body Shop."

"You serious?"

Ellen nodded grimly.

"I've got an idea. Let's leave the mall and walk to the Starbucks on North Michigan Avenue. If he follows us all the way down there, we'll know for sure it's not a coincidence."

When the two women arrived at Starbucks ten minutes later, their cheeks were stinging from the cold. Bertie rubbed her hands together and stomped her feet as she contemplated the menu.

"What do you think," she said, taking her place in line. "Should I get a chai latte or a regular one?"

But Ellen did not reply. Instead, she whirled abruptly to confront a nondescript black man wearing a North Face ski jacket.

"What are you, some kind of pervert?" she said, wagging a finger in the man's face. "If you don't stop following me right now, I'm calling the police."

The man smiled thinly. "I don't think that will be necessary, Professor Simpson." He reached into his jacket pocket and flipped open his wallet. "Mervyn Tollis, FBI. Let's sit down and talk, shall we?"

"Hold on just a minute," Bertie said. Whipping out her cell phone, she punched in Big Mac's number, but no one picked up. Frustrated, she left a desperate message as Tollis took Ellen gently by the elbow and steered her to an empty table.

"Your friend is not under suspicion for anything," Tollis said. "I just want to ask her a few questions." With exaggerated courtesy, he pulled out a chair and gestured for Ellen to sit down. But when Bertie moved to join them, he said, "This is just between Professor Simpson and myself. It won't take long."

"Go on home, Bertie. I'll take a cab. If I don't talk now, this man will just keep following me." As Bertie looked on helplessly, Ellen flashed Tollis a challenging glare, disdaining the chair the agent had selected, and sat down on the other side of the table. "Okay, hotshot. Let's get this over with. You've got ten minutes."

For the next four hours, Bertie called Big Mac's home number every five minutes, but there was no response. Nor did he answer the phone at his office. Frustrated, she fired him off an email and a pair of text messages. What on earth could the man be doing in the middle of the day? Wasn't he checking his messages?

Suddenly, a memory from her not-so-distant past hit her like a hammer. Around this time every Saturday, she and Delroy had locked the door, closed the curtains, and turned off the phone.

"Mmm, baby," he'd whisper, kissing the nape of her neck, "I got all afternoon. C'mon and give me some sugar."

The memory of her husband's hands moving gently along her body was so visceral it hurt. For some strange reason, the idea of Mac and Angelique engaged in a similar activity was almost as painful. Try as she might, Bertie could not forget how comforting Mac's hand had felt against her own. Almost against her will, she recalled how Mac's eyes had gentled when he looked at her. What a beautiful man he was—strong, yet sweet at the same time. What would it be like to hear him say *C'mon baby—give me some sugar?*

"Stop that this instant, Bertie Bigelow," she said in a loud, firm voice.

She stood up and put a fresh kettle of water on to boil, punching in Mackenzie's number as she waited. When Mac did not pick up, she hung up without leaving a message and tried Ellen's cell phone. It was nearly nine o'clock. Ellen should have finished her meeting with Agent Tollis hours ago.

Normally, tea had a soothing effect on Bertie, but today, it did nothing but make her restless and irritable. Resolutely putting images of giving or receiving "sugar" out of her mind, she grabbed her coat and strode out the door. She should never have left Ellen alone with that FBI man. For all Bertie knew, the Feds could have stuffed her best friend into a helicopter and shipped her to Guantanamo. Not likely, but still.

Thirty minutes later, she parked her car in the bus stop down the street from Starbucks and ran inside. But Ellen and Agent Tollis were nowhere to be seen. The barista at the counter remembered them, however.

"They left here about three hours ago," she said.

"Together?"

"Definitely," the girl replied. "Your friend waited while the man came over and gave me a big tip."

Stumped, Bertie ran back to her car, pulling it out just as a meter maid, dressed to withstand the biting Chicago wind in multiple layers of heavy clothing, lumbered purposefully in her direction. Bertie tried Ellen's number four more times on her way back to the South Side, but there was no answer. What on earth could have happened?

On a whim, she turned off Outer Drive at 31st Street. Ellen's apartment was right on Bertie's way home. The least she could do was to check to see if Ellen was okay. It was entirely possible Ellen had been so traumatized by her FBI interview that she was brooding alone in her apartment this very minute. Unlike the North Side, where parking spaces were at a premium, there was plenty of space in front of Ellen's Bronzeville apartment building. Built at the turn of the last century, the venerable stone building had once been the home of a wealthy Chicago hog butcher before being purchased by an African American real estate mogul in the 1940s. While the fortunes of the surrounding neighborhood had waxed and waned, Ellen's building had remained solidly middle class—a haven for teachers, doctors, and, lately, young white couples looking for affordable real estate.

She parked her car and ran up the steps. Fortunately for Bertie, someone—undoubtedly a yuppie unacquainted with the rigors of inner city living—had left the door to the building's elegant foyer propped open. Visions of her friend alone and immobilized by depression flashed through Bertie's mind as she ran up the three flights of stairs leading to Ellen's apartment. She was just about to bang on the door when she heard laughter coming from inside.

"You are too much, Mervyn. Can I get you another rum and Coke?" Ellen's voice was unmistakable, and far from sounding traumatized, she was clearly enjoying herself.

"Don't mind if I do," Bertie heard the FBI agent reply. "Can't have my prime suspect out-drinking me, can I?"

As Bertie tiptoed back down the stairs, she couldn't decide whether to laugh or scream. She'd been in a lather of worry, picturing Ellen in jail or worse. Instead, her best friend had managed to get along just fine without her.

As usual.

When Ellen called the next morning to recount her adventures, Bertie pretended to be surprised.

"Turns out Mervyn's a real sweetheart, Bert. He's from Mississippi, just like me, only he's from way down in Biloxi—a real down-home Southern gentleman, smooth as velvet."

"So I take it you are no longer under suspicion of whatever it was he was following you for?"

"Of course not," Ellen said. "Raquib, however, is in deep doo-doo."

After leaving Starbucks, Mervyn Tollis had taken Ellen to a scandalously expensive dinner at Alinea Restaurant on his FBI expense account. Over dessert and brandy, he'd shown her surveillance photos of Raquib selling fake passports to an undercover agent.

"The only reason the FBI hasn't busted him yet is they want to see if there are any other conspirators," Ellen said. "That's why Mervyn was following me. But once we got that mess sorted out, we had a lovely evening."

"I thought Raquib was the love of your life."

"True," Ellen said. "But that was before I found out about his criminal activities. In retrospect, I should have figured he was up to something sketchy. One minute, he'd be all lovey and romantic. The next minute, he'd clam up tighter than a tick in January. He got dozens of phone calls every day, yet when I'd ask to meet his friends, he'd put me off with some lame excuse or other."

"So you dumped him?"

"No need. By tomorrow he'll be in Federal custody."

"And you're okay with this? I thought you hated all Feds on general principle."

"Well, you know how it is, Bertie. There are exceptions to every rule, especially where love is concerned."

"Love? Don't tell me you've hooked up with this Mervyn character already."

"Of course not," Ellen said haughtily. "My mama raised me better than that. However, I am considering it. If Mervyn plays his cards right, that is. But enough about me. You heard anything new from the police about LaShawn's case?"

Bertie told Ellen about the entries she'd read in LaShawn's notebook.

"Sounds like kid fantasy stuff to me, Bert. Secret Agent 005, my black behind. Crazy old Theophilous just roped the kid in to his loony, paranoid head trip. Have you talked to anybody else about this?"

"I've been blocked at every turn," Bertie said. "Detective Kulicki hasn't returned my calls, and neither has Mac. When I thought you'd been kidnapped by the FBI, I emailed, texted, and left a bunch of messages, but he still hasn't gotten back. Mac must still be mad at me for bothering him at work the other day." Bertie sighed. "Still, I promised Mrs. Petty I would do what I could. The choir is singing at LaShawn's funeral tomorrow. If Mac is there, I'll try to talk to him again."

"Be sure you talk to both him *and* Detective Kulicki."

Chapter Twenty-Six

Rock of Ages Pentecostal Tabernacle was located in a brick storefront at the corner of 71st and Ashland Avenue, not far from where LaShawn had lived with his grandmother. Purple velvet drapes covered the two large plate-glass windows facing the street. A large neon cross hung over the entrance, casting a pale radiance over the stream of mourners entering the building.

At the front of the church, LaShawn's casket sat on a small platform, surrounded by a bevy of flowers. As a wizened usher in a threadbare black suit led Bertie and her choir to a row of folding chairs just behind the casket, she spotted several familiar faces. Metro College was closed for the President's Day holiday, and a large contingent of students and faculty had turned out to honor LaShawn's memory. Uncharacteristically attired in a conservative black suit and matching pumps, Ellen waved discreetly as Bertie passed by. Maria Francione, decked out in a flamboyant red hat, sat next to Letitia Petrowski in the third row. This was probably the first time the chemistry teacher had ever been in a room with this many black people. She sat on the edge of her chair, as if ready to bolt at the first sign of trouble. Next to her, Jack Ivers, rumpled as always in an ancient tweed sports jacket, stared stoically into the distance.

At the back of the church, Dr. Humbert Grant and Alderman Steady Freddy Clark stood alongside Bishop Morris Norwood, the pastor of the church. All three men wore somber faces and black suits. As Bertie and her choir took their seats, Dr. Grant caught her eye. Although he said nothing, Bertie knew what he was thinking. If anything out of line happened during this performance, contract or no contract, she'd be out of a job before morning. She nodded crisply in his direction and sat down.

To Bertie's great relief, Patrice Soule and Charley Howard were nowhere to be seen. Bertie was even more relieved when she spotted David Mackenzie in the corner, huddled in conversation with Detective Kulicki. As soon as the service was over, she planned to corral the two men and dig out some more information.

In the last row, Dr. Momolu Taylor, dressed in an embroidered, purple robe and gold kufi hat, sat talking to Jawann Peters, who wore a black gabardine suit. When the two men looked at their funeral programs, Bertie covertly studied their faces to gauge their reaction to the full-page advertisement she'd taken out on the clinic's behalf:

IN LOVING MEMORY OF
LASHAWN VICTOR THOMAS
FROM HIS FRIENDS AT
THE PRINCETON AVENUE
NATURAL HEALTH CLINIC
AND
UPWARD RISE YOUTH SERVICES

Our joys will be greater
Our love will be deeper
Our lives will be fuller
Because we shared your moment

To the right of LaShawn's casket, an elderly man picked up a battered electric guitar and began to play. He was soon joined by an equally elderly woman who slapped a tambourine rhythmically against her thigh as she sang.

By and by, by and by
I'm gonna lay down
This heavy load

I know my robe's gonna fit me well
I tried it on at the gates of hell

By and by, by and by
I'm gonna lay down this heavy load

When the woman finished singing, she sat down to a chorus of amens from the congregation, and after a lengthy prayer, the minister invited Dr. Humbert Grant to come to the pulpit. As Grant addressed the congregation in his usual ponderous style, LaShawn's grandmother, attired in a shapeless black dress, watched bleakly from her seat in the first row. Although a large black hat covered most of her face, Mrs. Petty's cheeks were wet with tears. It had been barely a year since LaShawn's father had been killed attempting to rob a liquor store. Bertie could not even begin to imagine how hard it would be to lose a second family member to violence in such a short span of time. LaShawn's sister, Sherelle, sat next to Mrs. Petty. Unlike her grandmother, Sherelle was casually dressed in a pair of tightfitting pants and a black pullover.

As Dr. Grant continued to speak, she wept copiously, daubing her eyes and blowing her nose with a balled-up Kleenex. Sherelle had put the gun LaShawn had gotten from Peters in the glove compartment of her SUV. When the police went to look for the gun, however, it had mysteriously disappeared. Had this been the gun that killed Judge Green? LaShawn had insisted that Sherelle's car had been burglarized and the gun stolen. Remembering the promise she'd made to Mrs. Petty, Bertie prayed that LaShawn had in fact been telling the truth. The boy was innocent—he just had to be. No one as sweet, smart, and talented as LaShawn Thomas could actually shoot another human being in cold blood. Could they?

After Dr. Grant's eulogy, it was time for Bertie's choir to perform. Solemn and somber in their blue choir robes, the Metro Community College Singers formed two rows in front of LaShawn's casket. When her students were all in position, Bertie stood in front of them and raised her arms. As she brought them down, the choir began to sing:

Deep river
My home is over Jordan
Deep river
I want to cross over into campground

As the last mournful tones of the song faded away, there was a moment of silence. With a lump in her throat, Bertie signaled for the group, many of whom were now sobbing, to file back to their seats.

Two hours later, Lashawn Thomas's casket was carried out of the church by Tayquan, Ranaldo, and four other young men from the Englewood Upward Rise Program. They slid the coffin carefully into a long black hearse and stood silently at attention as the car drove off in the direction of the funeral home. The cremation that followed would be a private ceremony for just the family.

As Bertie stood on the sidewalk in front of the church, she spotted Dr. Momolu Taylor and Steady Freddy Clark huddled in conversation on the other side of the street. Oblivious of the frigid winter cold, the two men stood inches apart, engaged in what looked like an intense argument. As Bertie continued to observe them, the alderman suddenly shook his head, whirled on his heel, and strode off in the opposite direction. *Interesting*, Bertie thought to herself. Steady Freddy had nothing but praise for Dr. Momolu Taylor ten days ago. But it appeared that the two men had come to a distinct parting of the ways. As she pondered this new development, David Mackenzie appeared at her side.

"Didn't I tell you to stop meddling?" Big Mac took Bertie firmly by the elbow and led her away from the crowd. "My answering service got a call from the Hot Sauce King this morning. He wants me to help him sue you for defamation of character. He says you've accused him of murder twice this month. What the hell have you been up to?"

"If you follow me back to my place I can explain everything," Bertie said.

"Can you at least give me a hint?"

Out of the corner of her eye, Bertie caught Jawann Peters watching from across the street.

"I don't feel comfortable talking in the street like this. It won't take too long, I promise."

Mac studied her silently for a full minute before responding.

"You'd better have a damn good explanation ready. I'll meet you at your place in twenty minutes."

When Bertie was three blocks from home, she noticed a phalanx of emergency lights flashing at the corner of 57th and Harper. As she got closer, she began to smell smoke. One of the buildings on her block was on fire. Had something happened to the O'Fallon sisters? The two women were in their eighties. Perhaps they'd inadvertently left a space heater running too long. During Chicago's brutal winter season, these things happened all the time.

Bertie pulled her car to the curb and got out. Oblivious to the wind and the cold, she ran down Harper Avenue and pushed her way through the crowd of spectators lined up across the street from the burning building. Only then did she realize that it was not the O'Fallon's home that was burning.

"Oh my God," Bertie screamed and ran across the street toward the fire. "That's my house!"

Almost immediately, a fireman carrying an axe blocked her way and gestured for her to turn around.

"Stay on the other side of the street, ma'am," he said. "It's not safe here."

Chapter Twenty-Seven

With a sinking heart, Bertie watched the water from the fire hoses arc through the frigid air and cascade through her basement window. When David Mackenzie took her gently by the arm, she stared at him uncomprehendingly.

"Wait here," he said. "I'll find out what's going on." He shouldered his way through the crowd of onlookers and disappeared.

"Ah! Here ya are. At last!" Clad only in a housedress, a thick woolen sweater, and a pair of rubber galoshes, Pat O'Fallon materialized at her elbow. "Collie and I have been waitin' for ya since the conflagration started."

As clouds of inky smoke billowed from her basement window, Bertie brushed away a tear.

"She's looking mighty peaked." Colleen took hold of Bertie's other elbow.

"Of course she's looking peaked, ya idjit," Pat snapped. "Her house is burning down!"

She reached into the pocket of her overcoat and produced a small silver flask.

"Here luv," Pat said, patting Bertie solicitously on the arm. "Have a little taste. 'Twill calm the nerves."

Numbly, Bertie took the flask and lifted it to her mouth. As the whiskey warmed her belly, she felt her strength returning. As minutes

161

passed and it became apparent that the fire was not going to spread any further, the crowd of spectators began to disperse. Slowly, the flames turned to sizzling piles of ashes. Soon even Pat and Collie O'Fallon had retreated indoors.

Once the fire was out, the men, spent from their battle, collected their tools and rolled up their hoses. Bertie and Mac were the only onlookers left when the fire captain approached.

"We were able to confine the fire to the basement," he said. "It could have been a whole lot worse."

"Do you have any idea how it started?" Mackenzie asked.

"Not yet. Our investigator will contact Mrs. Bigelow in the next day or two."

Bertie had been standing outside in below zero weather for nearly two hours, dressed only in the fur coat and the thin silk dress she'd worn to LaShawn's funeral. Her head was spinning, and the whole experience had a surreal quality. Perhaps, if she pinched herself hard, she'd wake to discover that this whole situation had been a dream. She rubbed her hand across her face and closed her eyes. But when she opened them, the fire captain was still standing in front of her.

"How long will it be until Mrs. Bigelow can get inside her home?" Mackenzie said.

"It's going to take a while for us to finish up here," the captain said. "When we're sure the fire is completely out, I'll have my men board up the basement window. She ought to be able to get in there tomorrow."

"Tomorrow?" Numb from the cold and from the shock, Bertie bit her lip and stared at the ground.

"You need to get out of the cold," Mackenzie said. "Let's get some coffee while the men are finishing up here." He took Bertie's elbow and led her down the street.

Ten minutes later, over coffee at a table in Valois Cafeteria on 53rd Street, Mac said, "I hate to be the bearer of more bad news, but there's something we've got to talk about."

As she warmed her hands against her coffee cup, Bertie could feel herself coming back to life. Thank God the fire had been confined to the basement. Hopefully, her Steinway grand piano in the living room upstairs had not been damaged.

"Charley Howard is coming to see me tomorrow morning. He's hiring me to sue you for slander. If I can tell him you are sincerely sorry for any damage you may have done to his reputation, maybe I can convince him to drop the matter." Mac paused and looked Bertie in the eye. "Of course, you'll have to stop acting so foolish. What were you thinking, accusing him of murder like that?"

If there was one thing Bertie hated, it was being called foolish.

"You can tell Charley Howard to stick his stupid lawsuit where the sun doesn't shine," she said irritably. "The man is a bona fide murder suspect. He's got an arrest record, a violent temper, and violent friends. I saw him get into a ferocious argument with Judge Green at the Octagon Gala. What's more, he's not telling the truth about where he went the night of the murder. How do I know this? Because LaShawn Thomas saw him outside the judge's apartment at one thirty that morning."

When Bertie Bigelow finished, Mac took a deep breath and leaned back in his chair.

"If this stuff checks out, the Hot Sauce King should consider himself lucky not to have been arrested," he said. "But you've got to stop poking around in this thing. How many times do I have to tell you? Let the police handle this."

"I was *trying* to get the police involved, Mac. I left Detective Kulicki several messages, but he never phoned back. What was I supposed to do?"

"I spoke to the detective at the funeral this afternoon. He says he's working on a new lead. I know it doesn't seem like it, but the wheels of justice are grinding forward. In the meantime, please, stop meddling, and let the professionals do their job. You could be putting yourself in real danger. Has it occurred to you that someone may have set that fire on purpose?"

As a matter of fact, it had. In the upside-down fantasy her life had become, anything was possible. Murder? Arson? Just one more day in the life of Bertie Bigelow, amateur detective. On the one hand, she was terrified. But at the same time, in a strange and totally inexplicable way, Bertie felt more alive than she had in years. While nothing would ever bring LaShawn back to life, she could at least bring LaShawn's killer to justice. After all, she'd promised Mrs. Petty she'd look into things. Giving up now was just not an option.

"Do you have a place to stay tonight?" Mac said. "You're welcome to stay with Angelique and me. We've got a nice spare bedroom."

Bertie thanked him with a wan smile. "I'm a bit shell-shocked right now, but Ellen lives just ten minutes away. I'll give her a call."

"You sure you're okay?" Mac said. He pushed aside his cup and touched her gently on the arm. "Sorry I snapped at you earlier. But you worry me, putting yourself in danger like this."

Bertie stared down at the table, hoping that Mac did not notice how red her cheeks had become.

"No really, Mac. I'm fine. Go on home to your wife. She must be wondering where you are by now."

Mac sighed. "These days, I honestly don't know what Angie's thinking half the time." He pushed back his chair and stood up. "But that's another story. The important thing at the moment is to keep you safe and sound." He leaned down and kissed her gently on the forehead. "Promise me you'll keep out of this, Bertie. If something ever happened to you, I don't know what I'd do. I care a lot about you."

Chapter Twenty-Eight

MONDAY, FEBRUARY 18, 2013—9:00 P.M.

The minute Bertie walked into Ellen's apartment, she was given a tall glass, filled to the brim with coconut rum.

"Drink this straight down," Ellen ordered. "It'll settle your nerves."

Instructing Bertie to take a seat on the couch, Ellen turned up the heat full blast and bustled off to find sheets for the futon in her spare bedroom.

"Tell me what happened," Ellen hollered from the next room over the soft jazz playing on the stereo.

"I don't know what happened," Bertie hollered back. "The good news is that the fire started in the basement and did not spread through the rest of the house. I'll find out more tomorrow. Apparently, the fire department is still investigating."

Ellen, who had changed out of her black suit into an orange kente cloth muumuu, strode back into the living room and stood in front of Bertie with her hands on her hips.

"What do you mean, investigating? Do they think it might be arson or something?"

Bertie shrugged. "All the man said is that they are investigating, and that I can't go home until tomorrow."

"Seems like the universe has decided to turn our little world completely upside down," Ellen said. She poured herself a double shot of rum and plopped down on the couch. "First, the judge gets killed. Then, LaShawn. And now this fire? I don't want to think about what could happen next."

"Mac says the police have a new lead in the case. Personally, I'll believe it when I see it." Bertie sipped her drink slowly, allowing the warmth of the rum to flow through her body. "He read me the riot act tonight. Told me to stop meddling in police business and leave the whole thing alone. But I promised LaShawn's grandmother I would try to find out what happened, and I am going to keep my word."

"Mac is one fine man, Bert."

"Reminds me of one of those Saint Bernard dogs," Bertie said. Despite everything that had happened in the last twenty-four hours, she found herself smiling. "You know, the big fuzzy ones they use to rescue people?"

"David Mackenzie can rescue me any time," Ellen said.

"He kissed my forehead and said he was worried about me."

"Bet he wanted to kiss more than that," Ellen said. Bertie flushed but remained silent. "Come on, Bertie. You're not a married woman anymore. It's time to reawaken your natural feminine radar. Can't you see the man's got a thing for you?"

Bertie drew herself erect. "I may not be married, but Mac sure is." She polished off the rum in her glass and set it decisively on the table. "I'll admit I'm lonely. But I'll never be any good at flirting, reading signals, all that crap."

"Baby, these are skills you can learn," Ellen said. "And lucky for you, you are in the presence of a master. Here. Have another drink while I school you."

"Gonna tell me how you seduced that FBI agent?" Bertie giggled wickedly. "And speaking of seduction, how are things with Raquib? Has he called you from jail?"

"I thought Raquib was going to be The One." Ellen sighed and took another long swallow from her glass. "We had history, Raquib and I. Shared memories of a golden time in my life. But the man is a hardened criminal. I've got to admit, he fooled me, Bertie."

Bertie sipped her drink in silence. She saw no use in pointing out that Ellen's vaunted feminine radar had clearly failed in this instance.

"Fate has a way of evening things out, though," Ellen continued. "If it hadn't been for Raquib, there would never have been Mervyn." She splashed another shot of rum into her glass and smacked her lips lasciviously. "The man doesn't talk much, but when I finally let him in my bed, I just know he's gonna sing me a pretty song."

"This is exactly what I'm talking about," Bertie said. "I could never in my wildest dreams imagine dealing with that many men in the space of a single week."

"I'm not suggesting you try," Ellen said. "Got to walk before you can run. I was simply pointing out that David Mackenzie—an attractive, intelligent, and honorable man—has the hots for you."

"Mac *is* attractive, intelligent, and honorable. But he's also *married*, Ellen."

"For the moment, my friend. For the moment." Ellen's bracelets jingled merrily as she picked up her glass and took a long swallow. "My girlfriend Kathy saw Angelique Mackenzie getting pretty cozy with one of the musicians at The Loft last weekend. Kathy says the girl was drunk as a skunk to boot. Something tells me the sanctity of marriage may not be at the top of her priority list."

"Poor Mac," Bertie said softly. "No wonder he looked so tired."

"All the man needs is a little lovin' to put him right. And you are just the person to do it."

Bertie flushed deep red. Tears stung her eyes as she glared across the coffee table at her best friend.

"That's enough, Ellen. Enough. I don't want to talk about this anymore. I am just not in the mood, okay?"

Ellen held up her hands in surrender. "I was only teasing, Bertie. Trying to cheer you up a little. But you're right, let's change the subject." She lifted the bottle of coconut rum off the coffee table in front of her and splashed another shot into their glasses. "Does it seem like we're living in the middle of a Miss Marple episode lately?"

As Bertie smiled wanly, Ellen crossed her legs primly.

"So tell me, Miss Detective," she said in an absurdly aristocratic English accent. "Who really killed Judge Theophilous Green?"

Bertie giggled and took another sip of rum. "I'm no Miss Marple, girlfriend. I'm just trying to figure out what happened. I promised LaShawn's grandmother I would look into it."

"I know," Ellen said in her regular voice. "So seriously. If LaShawn didn't do it, the killer is probably someone else we know. Was it Charley Howard?"

"Could have been. Charley was at the Jackson Towers the night Judge Green was killed. LaShawn saw him there. He threatened to tell the cops he'd seen Charley outside the Judge's apartment unless Charley got him an appointment with Tony Roselli."

"But LaShawn was no hoodlum," Ellen said. "Why would he want to meet with a Mob boss?"

"No one knows for sure, of course. But I think LaShawn stumbled onto something big the night he was killed. That's what he told Letitia Petrowski just hours before his death."

Ellen grunted. "Don't tell me Petrowski killed him. I'll slap the handcuffs on the dilly heifer myself."

For the first time all day, Bertie burst out laughing. What a blessing it was to have a friend she could tell her troubles to. Sure, Ellen teased her a bit too much. But even this was probably a good thing. The last person Bertie wanted to become was a humorless stick-in-the-mud.

"Remember the isopropyl nitrite I told you about?" Bertie continued between giggles. "LaShawn called Petrowski because he wanted to find out if the drug was legal. I'm thinking LaShawn found that stuff at the clinic and didn't know what to do with it."

Ellen whistled softly. "A cache of illegal drugs at the Princeton Avenue Natural Health Clinic. Wouldn't that be something?"

"It would indeed. I know it sounds farfetched, but Dr. Taylor likes to push the rules. He's got Patrice Soule so hopped up on diet pills she's damn near lost her mind." Bertie picked up the bottle of rum from the coffee table and refilled her glass. "And as long as we're talking murder suspects, let's not omit Patrice Soule, Chicago's Next New Thing. She told me herself that she owns a nine millimeter handgun. And when the judge tried to get frisky with her, she threatened him with it."

"Sick of having the old creep follow her around, no doubt," Ellen said. "Did you ever think that the judge's murder could have been an accident? Soule might have been so revved up on speed that her trigger finger just slipped."

Bertie shook her head. "If Patrice is the killer, I'm guessing she knew what she was doing. The woman's got a temper on her. I wouldn't be surprised if she's pulled that gun on Dr. Taylor a time or two."

Ellen, who'd gone into the kitchen to forage for more solid food to balance the bottle of rum they were working themselves through, returned with a bag of taco chips and a jar of salsa.

"It's funny, though," Ellen said as she poured them each another drink. "I keep thinking how much the doctor resembles this guy I had a crush on back in Jackson."

"Have you always had boys on the brain?"

"So it would seem," Ellen replied merrily. "Just the way I'm built, I guess. This was pure puppy love, though. I was ten, and he was already in high school. Tommy Ponder. I'm sure he didn't even know I existed. I don't know why, but every time I see Momolu Taylor, I think about him."

"Maybe the doctor's got relatives in Jackson. Did you ever ask him?"

"Nah," Ellen said, shaking her head. "When I get around Momolu Taylor, I lose my train of thought completely. That is a man with a lot of animal magnetism. Don't tell me your heart doesn't flutter a little when he stands too close. The man may sell a dick stiffener, but something tells me he doesn't need one, if you get my drift."

"If anyone should know about these kind of things, I guess it would be you," Bertie said, laughing. "You might be right about the virility thing, though. Before he moved to the States, the doctor kept a harem of four teenaged wives. Says he's related to Togar Henries, the Liberian diamond magnate."

"Get outta here. Where on earth did you dig that up?"

"Delroy wrote about it in his manuscript." Bertie dug a taco chip out of the bag and popped it into her mouth. "I don't know if it's really true, though. Judge Green told Delroy to re-check Taylor's citizenship papers. I was going to ask the doctor about it when I saw him at the Loft."

"Why didn't you?"

Bertie blushed. "I guess I forgot. Tell you the truth, I was having a hard time concentrating."

"See what I mean?" Ellen cackled. "That man could charm the drawers off Mother Theresa."

"Don't be ridiculous. No man is going to pull the wool over my eyes like that." As Ellen collapsed on the couch in a heap of giggles, Bertie picked up the bottle of rum and waved it in the air to emphasize her point. "You think I'm lying? Just watch me. I'm going to call him up right now and ask him."

Shaking with laughter, Ellen grabbed the bottle out of Bertie's hand.

"No more rum for you, my sister."

Maybe Ellen was right. Bertie did notice the room was beginning to spin. Still, the thought that she had allowed herself to be flummoxed by the doctor's charms irritated her.

"The doctor could be hiding something. I could feel him tense up when I told him about Delroy's memoir."

Ellen slapped her thighs and howled with laughter. She lurched to her feet and wobbled on unsteady legs into the spare room. After several minutes of banging and clattering sounds, she emerged triumphantly, carrying her cell phone.

"You think Taylor is hiding something? Why don't we call the brother and ask him?"

"How do you think he'd handle it?" Bertie said. "Would he act all indignant or play it cool?"

"Girl, you know he'd be smooth as velvet. An African Denzel Washington."

Like a pair of schoolgirls at a slumber party, the two women giggled at the thought of rattling the unflappable doctor. Taking another swallow of rum from her glass, Ellen found the doctor's number, hit the "call" button, and thrust the phone into Bertie's hand.

"Oh my God! I can't believe you did that!" Bertie squealed. "Quick. Hang up!"

But it was too late.

"You have reached the office of Dr. Momolu Taylor at the Princeton Avenue Health Clinic," the doctor's voice purred. Even on the tinny speakers of Ellen's cell phone, he sounded sexy. "I'm away from the office, but if you leave me a message, I will return your call."

Thank God it was the answering machine. Bertie could have hung up. But, perhaps due to the fact that she had now consumed nearly half a bottle of rum on an empty stomach, she decided to leave a message instead. Pulling herself up, she spoke carefully and clearly into the telephone.

"Dr. Taylor, this is Bertie Bigelow. As I told you when we met at The Loft, I am thinking of having my husband's memoir published. Delroy wrote a nice profile on you, but he had some questions I was hoping you could help me with. Something about your citizenship papers?" Despite her best intentions to sound professional, Bertie hiccupped. "Oops. Sorry about that. One more thing. Are you related to any people named Ponder? My girlfriend swears she knows a guy who looks just like you. Please give me a call at your earliest convenience."

As Bertie hung up the phone and set it on the coffee table, Ellen roared with laughter.

"At your earliest convenience? Negro, are you kidding me? Your mama sho 'nuff taught you some manners."

"Now look what you made me do, Ellen! What can I possibly say when the man calls me back?"

"We'll cross that bridge when we come to it," Ellen said. She waved her hands grandly in the air, like the Pope blessing a supplicant. "Our work here is done, my child. Let's call Harold's Chicken Shack and order some wings."

For the rest of the evening, Bertie and Ellen drank rum, pigged out on fried chicken, and watched bad movies on TV. Neither woman said another word about Bertie's fire, the murders, Dr. Momolu Taylor, or the Hot Sauce King. By the time Bertie collapsed in a soggy stupor on the futon in Ellen's spare room, she was feeling no pain.

Chapter Twenty-Nine

TUESDAY, FEBRUARY 19, 2013—7:00 A.M.

Bertie awoke with a start, heart pounding as she surveyed her unfamiliar surroundings. It took a minute to adjust to her new reality. *Ah, yes. I'm at Ellen's. Ah, yes. I've been burned out of my home. Ah, yes.*

She glanced over at the alarm clock on the end table. It was early—seven a.m. The sun was just beginning to fight through the leaden gray clouds outside. Ellen, a notoriously late sleeper, did not have to teach at Metro College until the afternoon. As for herself, Bertie knew there was no way she would be able to go to work that day. She dug her cell phone out of her purse and left a quick message on Hedda Eberhardt's answering machine, cancelling her classes for the day and explaining about the fire. Although her absence was likely to get her in more hot water with Dr. Grant, Bertie would just have to deal with that situation later. She still had three weeks to make her case before the faculty disciplinary committee met to review her conduct at the Christmas concert. Hopefully, by that time her life would have become a bit less chaotic.

As she collected her clothes and folded Ellen's futon back into its regular position, Bertie mulled over her options. She could sit around her friend's apartment for another several hours waiting for her to wake up, or she could get dressed and go back to her house. The firemen had said she would be able to get into the place in the morning, and this was certainly morning.

Moving carefully on tiptoe, Bertie took a shower, got dressed, and gathered up the rest of her things. Then, on the coffee table next to the remains of last night's chicken dinner, she left a note to say she'd gone home. Pulling Ellen's door shut quietly behind her, Bertie wrapped her coat tightly around her shoulders and stepped outside into the cold. Thank goodness her trusty Toyota fired up immediately. As she waited for the engine to warm up, Bertie went over the mental "to do" list she'd composed for the day.

1) Meet with the fire marshal.
2) Call the insurance company.
3) Call the gas company and get the heat turned back on.
4) Call Dr. Momolu Taylor and apologize.

What was I thinking, calling up the doctor in the middle of the night talking trash? Bertie asked herself. *Honestly, this is absolutely the last time I drink hard liquor.*

As she pulled in front of her house, the fire marshal was already standing on her front porch, clipboard at hand. The man was tall and stoop-shouldered, with gray hair and an impish smile.

"My name is Abe Rattner," he said, bending down to shake her hand. "I've got good news, and I've got bad news. Which do you want to hear first?"

"Just give it to me straight," Bertie said tartly. "There's nothing to laugh about here."

The marshal's cheeks turned beet red. "My boss is always telling me to be less flippant when dealing with the public. Honestly, I was just trying to make you smile. Things go down so much better with a smile, don't you think?"

When he did not perceive even the glimmer of a smile on Bertie's face, Abe Rattner pulled out his clipboard, cleared his throat, and forged ahead.

"The good news is that you had the presence of mind to install a sprinkler system in your home. Thanks to your foresight, the damage was confined to the basement. The bad news is that this fire was no accident. But whoever did this was an amateur or they would have known to disable the system before starting the fire."

"Someone did this on purpose?" Bertie said. "Who would do such a thing?"

"Kids, probably. We found the remains of a plastic gasoline container down in the basement. Sad to say, we've seen a number of similar fires in your neighborhood over the past few months. I've notified the police. An officer from the bomb and arson unit should be in touch with you in the next day or so."

Bertie nodded bleakly.

"I've checked out your gas and electric lines. You should have electricity by this afternoon, and the gas company will send a man sometime today to restart your furnace. In the meantime, you're welcome to go inside, assess the damage, and contact your insurance company."

Without waiting for a response, Rattner tipped his hard hat and walked back down the stairs. As he got into his car and drove away, Bertie hesitated on her porch, reluctant to face the devastation she was sure to find inside. Though Ellen had nagged her repeatedly to purchase a security system, she'd never quite gotten around to it. Who needed a burglar alarm when you had the O'Fallon sisters next door? Apparently, she did. Despite her bedrock belief in the fundamental good nature of human beings, something evil had happened here, right in her own house.

Bertie took a deep breath, unlocked her front door, and stepped inside. Ignoring the acrid smell of smoke in the air and the burn marks on the walls, she raced upstairs to the music room. When she saw that her Steinway grand piano had survived, Bertie's heart soared. Thanks to the sprinkling system Delroy had convinced her to install, the instrument stood intact in the center of the room, its heavy plastic cover encased in a thin sheet of ice. Gently, she rolled back the cover and ran her finger over the keys. Severely out of tune, of course, from its unexpected encounter with the elements, but still functional.

CAROLYN MARIE WILKINS

Shivering in the cold, Bertie continued on to the third floor. Although her bedroom smelled faintly of smoke, she was relieved to discover that nothing had burned. She changed into a pair of old jeans, a sweatshirt, and a pair of work boots. Grabbing a pair of rubber gloves and a box of Hefty bags from the kitchen, she trudged down to the basement to inspect the damage. Although the room remained structurally intact, Delroy's African mask collection had been reduced to ashes along with his books and most of his files. Dragging an old electric heater out of the closet by the front door, Bertie hauled it downstairs and plugged it in. The fire marshal had promised her she'd have power before the end of the day. Sure enough, the heater sprang to life when she hit the "on" button, sending a small blast of warmth into the frigid room. Hopefully, someone from the gas company would arrive to turn on her furnace soon. In the meantime, Bertie was determined to get her house in some kind of order. After spending a minute rubbing her hands together, she began the unpleasant task of sorting through the debris scattered across the basement floor.

Two hours later, Bertie was throwing out the charred remains of what had once been Blackstone's Law Dictionary when a thin manila folder caught her eye. Despite the odds, at least one of Delroy's files had managed to survive the fire. Although much of it was missing, she could tell the file contained papers related to Dr. Momolu Taylor's biography. On a sheet of note paper, Delroy had written *check Taylor's status with USCIS* in red. Then he'd circled it.

What was USCIS anyway? Idly, she took out her iPhone and tapped the letters into her search engine. Instantly, the insignia of the United States Customs and Immigration Service filled the screen. Suddenly, her drunken prank of the night before seemed a lot less funny. What if Dr. Taylor really did have a secret to hide? Without proper papers, an African was likely to be deported in a heartbeat. Bertie began to comb through the jumble of papers on the floor with renewed intensity. But aside from a few scraps of paper from Taylor's libel suit against WLS radio, she found nothing more.

176

An hour later, the doorbell rang. For the next twenty minutes, a burly inspector from People's Gas went over her furnace and kitchen stove with a fine-tooth comb. When at last he pronounced them safe and turned her heat back on, Bertie nearly jumped for joy. As soon as he left, she fixed herself a hot cup of tea and continued sorting through the debris in the basement. The thought that the fire might have destroyed all the research Delroy had amassed in the course of writing his book was just too much to bear. Surely, she would be able to find something useful amid the debris.

It was nearly dark outside before she struck pay dirt. The scrap of paper was soggy and reeked of smoke, but it was still legible. Written in her husband's loopy scrawl, it was dated March 13, 2012, a week before his death.

Taylor Bio questions
Relation to Liberian elite—Henries family denies. Omit?
Clinic not listed w/ Lib. ministry. If no listing, omit.
Immigration—no nat. form on record—check w/
Theophilous. re legal implications

Clearly, Delroy had run into a series of problems trying to authenticate Dr. Taylor's history. Although the doctor claimed royal ancestry, the Emir of Kano denied it. What's more, the African clinic the doctor claimed to have founded was not listed with the Liberian Ministry of Health. Most damning, US Customs had no record of Taylor becoming an American citizen. Clearly Momolu Taylor was not the man he claimed to be, but what did any of this have to do with LaShawn finding isopropyl nitrite at the Princeton Avenue Clinic? Feeling overwhelmed and exhausted, Bertie swept another pile of sooty debris into a Hefty bag and carried it outside.

"How're ya farin' with the cleanup, Bertie?" Pat O'Fallon slammed her back door and bustled outside, an oversized trash bag in each hand. "Collie said we should come over and offer assistance, but

I said to let you be. Let Bertie have some time to grieve, I said." Spry as a teenager, despite her eighty-plus years, Pat O'Fallon lifted the lid of the large metal dumpster and flung her trash bags inside. "But now it's a hot meal you'll be wantin'. Collie's got a stew on the burner. Supper's in twenty minutes. Don't be late."

Ten minutes later, Bertie sat at the O'Fallon's retro Formica-topped kitchen table, nursing a hot cup of tea.

"We thought ya might need a little somethin' to keep yer strength up," Colleen warbled gaily. "What with the fire and all." Dressed in a pink nightgown, a blue chenille robe, a pair of men's black dress socks, and ratty gray mules, Colleen O'Fallon stood in front of the stove, stirring a black cast-iron pot with a wooden spoon. As the fragrant cooking smells hit her nostrils, Bertie's stomach growled appreciatively.

"Ya must be starvin'," Pat said. "How about a wee nip. You've had a long, cold day over there, I'll wager." Without waiting for a reply, the old woman reached for the bottle of Jameson Irish Whiskey standing on the counter and poured a splash into Bertie's tea.

"It has been a long day," Bertie said. "My entire basement is a shambles. Thank God the sprinklers came on. Otherwise, the whole house would've burned down."

After ladling a steaming portion of lamb stew onto each plate, Colleen wiped her hands on the dishtowel hanging next to the sink and sat down next to her sister.

"I knew those lads were trouble," she said. "Back in our school teaching days, we had a few of that sort, didn't we, Pat?"

"Right hooligans they were," Pat said.

"Lollygagging," Colleen said, waving her fork for emphasis. "Those boys. Actin' like they had nothin' better to do but stand 'round the corner in this freezin' weather."

"There were boys hanging around yesterday?" Bertie didn't want to snap at the two old women, but she did wish they would get to the point. "What kind of boys?"

"Black boys," Pat said. "I came out on the porch and gave 'em a good talking-to."

"Sure she did," Colleen said, spearing a potato with her fork. "And do you know what they said?"

"Such filthy mouths on the young people nowadays," Pat said, shaking her head. "Back in my school teachin' days, I'd a knocked some sense into 'em long before they got big enough to make mischief."

Bertie forgot all about her food.

"Let me get this straight. You saw a group of boys hanging around my house right before the fire?"

In a rare moment of harmony, both sisters nodded.

"I told them to push off, but they didn't," Pat said. "So I went back inside. I bolted my door, but I kept watching."

"We both kept watching," Colleen said. "When we saw the smoke coming out of your basement, we called 911 straightaway."

"Do you think you'd be able to recognize these boys if you saw them again?"

"They wore trainers with the laces untied and those baggy pants kids favor nowadays," Pat said.

"Tell her about the handkerchiefs," Colleen interjected.

"Handkerchiefs?" Bertie said. Once again, the O'Fallon sisters were talking in riddles.

"Not handkerchiefs, you idjit." Pat shook her head impatiently. "*Bandanas.*"

"Is that what they call the rags kids put on their heads?"

"Yes, Colleen," Bertie said grimly. "That's what they call them."

"Kids today don't have a grain of sense," Colleen said. "Wearin' a red rag in the middle of winter. What kind of rank idjit does such a thing?"

The Conquering Lions gang, that's who, Bertie thought. The Lions were the most powerful criminal organization on the South Side, and red bandanas were their signature fashion statement. People who got on the wrong side of the Conquering Lions often ended up in the morgue. Hoping the two sisters hadn't noticed the sudden pallor in her complexion, Bertie thanked the women for dinner and rushed home.

Chapter Thirty

Bertie locked and bolted her front door. Wearily, she climbed the stairs to the living room and sat down on the couch. Why would the South Side's most powerful street gang want to torch her home? If there was any good news, she supposed it was that the Conquering Lions were not trying to kill her. If they'd wanted, they could have shot her dead at any time. Apparently, they'd chosen to set her house on fire while she was out. Maybe the gang was trying to frighten her. If so, Bertie thought grimly, they had succeeded beyond their wildest dreams. Bertie pushed herself off the couch and had just begun to climb the stairs to her bedroom when she heard the doorbell ring.

Grabbing her purse, she pulled out her cell phone. If she did not see a familiar face at her front door, she'd call 911 immediately. Raising herself up on tiptoe, she squinted through the peephole. When she saw Detective Kulicki's pale face looking back at her, Bertie could not remember being happier to see anyone in her whole life. After inviting him inside, Bertie led him up to the kitchen.

"As you can see, someone set my house on fire," she told him, pointing out the burn marks and water stains that now lined her walls. "I think the Conquering Lions may be involved. My neighbors saw a bunch of kids wearing red bandanas hanging around the block just before the fire began."

As usual, the detective looked tired and rumpled. He had a bad case of five o'clock shadow and bags under his eyes.

"The Lions rarely engage in arson," Kulicki said. "Are you sure you don't know anyone associated with a gang? One of your students perhaps?"

"I've seen gang members hanging around the campus," Bertie said. "But not since Dr. Grant hired additional security guards. The only recent contact I've had with gangbangers were the ones I met when I visited the Upward Rise Program last week. Of course, that's the whole point of the program—to give the boys an alternative to the lives they've been living on the streets."

"I'm not so sure about that," Kulicki said. "I was on the gang task force before I transferred to homicide last year. Jawann Peters, the man who runs the program, has a criminal record as long as your arm. When Mr. Peters became assistant director at the Princeton Avenue Clinic, I warned Dr. Taylor about him. Obviously, the doctor chose to ignore me."

"Maybe Peters is using the clinic as a front for gang activity," Bertie said. "Before he was killed, LaShawn Thomas told the chemistry teacher at Metro College he'd found a case of isopropyl nitrite. I am betting that it came from Princeton Avenue Clinic."

"I'll check it out," Kulicki said. "If Peters was selling the drug for recreational use, he could be arrested. Have you spoken to anyone at the clinic since your visit last week?"

Bertie shifted uncomfortably in her seat. Now would be the time to tell Kulicki about the drunken message she'd left on Dr. Taylor's answering machine the night before. Though Detective Kulicki waited patiently, Bertie said nothing. How could she admit to this world-weary policeman that she had done something so incredibly stupid? After a full minute of silence, Kulicki closed his notebook and stood up.

"I'll have the division commander put an extra patrol car on your block," he said. "Be vigilant, Mrs. Bigelow. Your life is in danger."

After Detective Kulicki left, Bertie bolted the door, turned off all the lights, and climbed the stairs back to her bedroom. In spite of the fact that she had cranked the temperature in her house to nearly eighty degrees, she was shivering. Reaching up as high as she could, she felt along the back of her closet shelf. When she located the cardboard box containing her Smith & Wesson, she pulled it down and set it carefully on her bed. Her hands shook as she opened the box, extracted the gun, and shoved a round of bullets into the magazine. Years ago, her late husband had made her practice over and over until she could do it smoothly. Who would have thought she would ever have an occasion to load the gun again? Carefully, she slipped the loaded gun under her pillow before stripping off her clothes and climbing into bed.

For a few hours, she lay wide awake and stared at the ceiling while pictures of bandana-wearing youths raced through her mind. Finally, she swung her feet around and sat up. There was no way she was going to be able to sleep, at least not yet.

Ellen Simpson picked up the phone on the second ring. When Bertie told her that the O'Fallon sisters had seen kids wearing red bandanas in front of her house just before the fire, Ellen said, "If the Lions torched your house, they might come back to finish the job. You better stay at my place tonight."

"I refuse to let a bunch of hoodlums run me out of my own home," Bertie said. "I've got a gun under my pillow."

"Say what? I hope you're not seriously thinking about shooting somebody. Did you tell Detective Kulicki that you left a message on Taylor's machine last night?"

"I sort of omitted that part," Bertie said. "It makes me look like a complete idiot."

"Of course it does," Ellen said. "You should have told him anyway." She paused a moment, then said, "Suppose whoever burned your house down wanted you to think it was the Lions so they wore red bandanas. Or suppose it was someone else? Someone like the Roselli brothers, for instance?"

Bertie was silent as she absorbed this new possibility.

"Think about it," Ellen continued. "You've accused Charley Howard of murder twice. What if he didn't want to harm you, just scare you a little so you'd shut up and leave him alone? He could have paid some black kids to dress up like Lions and torch your house. Something like that would be child's play for mobsters like the Roselli brothers to arrange."

"I suppose they could have set the fire. Or, perhaps, it was set by a bunch of random kids who just happened to be wearing red bandanas."

"Perhaps," Ellen said slowly.

"Yeah, perhaps. The truth is, I just don't know."

"You want me to ask Mervyn to look into it? He could use his FBI connections to check it out. Unofficially, of course."

"No way," Bertie said. "I already feel like a complete idiot for getting myself into this mess. The last thing I need is to show up in some database somewhere."

"You sure? This is no time to be a hero, Bertie."

"I'll be fine," Bertie said. "Stop worrying so much. I'm scared enough as it is."

"That's why I should call Mervyn. Get you some protection."

"I've got protection," Bertie said firmly. "Detective Kulicki's putting an extra patrol car on my street."

"If you say so. But just in case, I'm keeping the phone right by my bed," Ellen said. "Call me if you need me, no matter what time it is." After making Bertie promise to check in first thing the following morning, Ellen hung up.

Although it was now nearly midnight, Bertie felt even less like sleeping than before. She clicked on the television and cycled absentmindedly through the channels. An hour later, after sitting through back-to-back reruns of *The Cosby Show*, Bertie was still wide awake.

On what seemed like her millionth trip to the bathroom that night, she peeked out of her bedroom window. Even though her rational mind told her it was unlikely the Lions would return, she could not stop herself from checking to see if anyone was lurking outside. When she saw a police cruiser drive slowly past the house, Bertie felt somewhat reassured and climbed back into bed. But despite the lateness of the hour, her body still refused to go to sleep. For the first time in her entire life, Bertie Bigelow was keeping a loaded gun under her pillow.

She kicked off the bedclothes and once again got out of bed. Since there was nothing on TV, maybe she'd be able to find a decent movie on Netflix. As she flipped open her laptop, Bertie got a devilish idea. Wouldn't it be something if she could dig up this Tommy Ponder dude Ellen was always babbling about? It would be fun to poke around on Google and see what turned up. Ellen, bless her heart, was totally computer phobic. It would never occur to her to search out her boyhood crush on the net. If Ellen had had better Googling skills, perhaps she could have avoided her most recent romantic debacle entirely. A quick search on CertifiedBackground.com revealed that Raquib Torrence had already been busted on fraud charges. It was nearly three in the morning, and Bertie had never been more wide awake in her life. If nothing else, Googling Ponder would provide a welcome distraction from her own problems.

Bertie tapped *Thomas Ponder* and *Mississippi* into her browser window. Five names turned up—four white men and an African American in his sixties. But caught up in the thrill of the hunt, she was not ready to give up. For the next hour she tried different spellings and combinations of variables. It wasn't until she added a "u" and "o" to Ponder's name that Bertie hit pay dirt—three newspaper articles from the *Woolworth Mississippi Tattler*.

NEW CLINIC BRINGS HOPE FOR RESIDENTS OF WOOLWORTH

May 4, 1998. Woolworth, MS—A groundbreaking ceremony for the Woolworth Natural Health Clinic will be held this Saturday at noon. Located at the corner of Fourth and Broad Streets, the clinic will specialize in alternative treatments, such as acupuncture, chiropractic, naturopathic, and herbal remedies. This project is the brainchild of Thomas Poundor and his wife, Olivia. Mrs. Poundor is a nurse with deep roots in Mississippi. Her father, George F. Hale, was the pastor of Banks Street AME Church in Tunica from 1955 to 1980.

"This clinic represents a lifelong dream," Mrs. Poundor told this reporter. "My husband and I intend to bring a new level of healthy living to this community."

At the bottom of the page, a dark-skinned black man and a slim, coffee-colored woman smiled optimistically as they pictured Woolworth's rosy future. The man in the photo bore a striking resemblance to Dr. Momolu Taylor. Of course, the man was younger and thinner, but in every other respect, the man could have been Taylor's twin.

Bertie's heart skipped several beats as she stared at the image before her. There was no way that a country doctor from Mississippi could resemble Momolu Taylor so closely unless the two men were the same. Eagerly, she scrolled down and clicked on the next article. It was dated June 15, 1999.

OLIVIA HALE POUNDOR, WIFE OF LOCAL DOCTOR, TAKES OWN LIFE

WOOLWORTH, MS—Mrs. Olivia Hale Poundor was pronounced dead at 2 p.m. yesterday afternoon at St. Dominic Hospital in Jackson. According to a spokesman for the hospital, Mrs. Poundor was admitted earlier in the day after having taken an overdose of Klonopin, a sedative often prescribed for people suffering from anxiety. Poundor's husband, Dr. Thomas Poundor, the director of the Woolworth Natural Health Clinic, stated that she had been taking the drug to treat an unspecified nervous condition for the past several months.

A memorial service for Mrs. Poundor will be held in Woolworth at St. Paul AME Church, 14 Gold Street, this Sunday at 3 p.m.

The third article was dated six months later.

NATURAL HEALTH CLINIC TO CLOSE

After numerous accusations of fraud and misman-agement, the Lincoln County Health Department has ordered the Woolworth Natural Health Clinic to close its doors pending an investigation into charges of fraud and mismanagement leveled against the clinic's founder, Dr. Thomas Poundor. According to an anonymous inside source, Poundor may be indicted soon on charges ranging from embezzlement to drug trafficking.

"Drug trafficking? Lord, have mercy," Bertie whispered as she read and reread the articles. Wrapping a quilt around her still shivering body, she reviewed the events of the last several days. Had Jawann Peters sent the Conquering Lions to burn her house down? Or had Charley Howard given up on his libel suit and decided to scare her into silence instead? What were the chances that Thomas Poundor and Momolu Taylor were actually the same man? Poundor's wife had died of a drug overdose. Had her death been an accident or a murder?

It was now nearly 5 a.m., too late to even think about going back to bed. Heaving a sigh, Bertie stumbled out of bed and into the shower. She'd taken yesterday off because of the fire, and as a result, two stacks of music history papers and last week's music appreciation listening exams sat ungraded on the battered metal desk in her office. The College would be quiet at this hour and she would be able to work without interruption. If she got started right away, she might even get her papers graded in time for her first class.

Thirty minutes later, Bertie Bigelow climbed into her Honda, popped a Stevie Wonder disc into the CD player, and headed along the dark and snow-covered Chicago streets toward Metro Community College.

Chapter Thirty-One

The campus was deserted. Bertie locked her car, wrapped a scarf around her neck, and zipped up her coat. As she strode briskly across the dark and deserted parking lot, it occurred to her that she probably should have waited for daylight before going out. But, of course, it was too late to worry about that now. She picked up her pace, singing the chorus of Stevie Wonder's "Livin' for the City" to bolster her courage. Once inside the building, she'd be perfectly safe. Every door except the main entrance was always kept locked. No one could gain access without swiping a college ID over the sensor by the door.

A sharp gust of wind raked Bertie across the face as she fumbled through her bag. *Mittens are probably not the ideal item to wear when searching for one's ID card*, she thought. Hunched against the cold, she continued to sing under her breath: "Livin' just enough, I'm livin' for the city . . ."

She was not aware of the man behind her until he grabbed her by the arm.

"I have a gun," he said. He poked her in the ribs with something sharp. "Keep walking, and act natural."

Bertie's first instinct was to scream. In a self-defense class she'd taken long ago, she'd learned that predators shy away from women that don't appear to be easy targets. But as she opened her mouth, the man clapped his hand over it.

"Shut up, bitch." The man twisted her arm behind her back and jammed the gun against her ribs. "Turn around and start walking."

The only sound Bertie could hear in the deserted parking lot was the crunch of their feet on the snow.

A large, black SUV with tinted windows rolled into the parking lot and glided to a stop in front of them. For a fleeting moment, Bertie thought someone, perhaps a campus security guard, was coming to investigate. But as she and her captor approached, two men in black pants, hoods, and ski masks jumped out of the car, tied her arms behind her back, and shoved her roughly onto the back seat. In a matter of seconds, Bertie was wedged next to the man with the gun.

"Who are you? Where are you taking me?" Her voice sounded tiny and very far away, as if it was coming from a small, wounded animal.

"Didn't I tell you to shut up?" The man slapped her across the face with the back of his hand. He leaned forward and spoke to one of the men seated in the front seat of the car. "Pass me that bottle of knock-out stuff, Damon. This bitch is getting on my last nerve."

With terrified eyes, Bertie watched as Damon leaned across the front seat to hand the man with the gun a small glass bottle and a towel.

"Give me the gun, OJ. I'll cover her while you take care of bizness."

OJ laughed roughly. "One hit of this shit and she ain't gonna need coverin'." He handed the gun to Damon, dumped the bottle's contents onto the towel, and shoved it over Bertie's face. The last thing she remembered before losing consciousness was OJ's twisted grin and the cloying scent of chloroform in her nostrils.

Chapter Thirty-Two

Bright light jolted Bertie Bigelow back to consciousness. As she twisted her head to avoid what felt like red pins exploding inside her eyeballs, she realized that she could neither scream nor move. Strips of duct tape sealed her mouth and bound her hands and feet. The harder she squirmed to try to free herself, the more tightly the tape bit into her wrists and ankles, while the unforgiving light continued to sear her eyeballs. As far as she could tell, she had been tied down to what felt like a metal operating table. The only sound in the room was the terrified pounding of her own heart.

Steady, girl. She forced herself to take a deep breath through her nose. *At least I'm still alive. If the man with the gun had wanted to kill me, I'd already be dead.* There was clearly no use struggling now. She would just have to wait and bide her time and be alert for a chance to escape. The cold metal table sent a chill up her spine, but Bertie forced herself to lie still. *Breathe in, breathe out.*

How long had she been lying there? Bertie fought through her clouded brain in an attempt to remember what had happened. Why would anyone want to kidnap her? She had no money to speak of, and she couldn't think of a single soul who would put up a significant amount of money for her ransom. As far as she knew, she had no enemies—except, of course, for whomever had torched her house. No enemies except for the cold-blooded killers who had murdered

191

Theophilous Green and LaShawn Thomas. As Bertie turned her head to the other side in an attempt to avoid the light's relentless glare, she realized that her kidnapping was, in some bizarre way, proof that these three events were related. The trouble was, everything that was happening seemed so surreal. Perhaps, in fact, she was simply dreaming. The pain behind her eyes made her doubt it.

Suddenly, Bertie heard footsteps coming closer and then the sound of a door opening.

"Good evening, Mrs. Bigelow," Dr. Momolu Taylor purred in a lilting baritone. Dressed in a set of blue surgical scrubs and cap, the doctor rubbed his hands together and smiled. "I trust my associates have made you comfortable?"

Bertie's heart rattled inside her chest. Why had she been brought here? She wanted to question the doctor, but the large strip of duct tape across her mouth made speech impossible. Instead, she turned her head and watched as Taylor wheeled a small metal stool up to the table where she lay.

Taking a seat, he called out, "Fetch me the bottle of J&B from my desk, Jawann. I believe this moment calls for a toast."

"Sure thing, boss." Although the doctor's assistant was out of her range of vision, Bertie recognized his gravelly voice immediately. Footsteps crossed the room, and the door opened then closed again. Although she was now beyond terrified, Bertie took a deep breath and willed herself to lie still. Whatever happened, she would not give Momolu Taylor the additional satisfaction of seeing her shake with fear. The door swung open a minute later.

"J&B, just like you wanted," Jawann Peters said. "Only brought glasses for you and me, though. Mrs. Bigelow looks a bit tied up at the moment."

Taylor laughed. "Fix me a drink, Jawann. Fix one for yourself, too, while you're at it. Tonight is a very special night."

From her position on the table, Bertie watched Peters fill a glass with whiskey and hand it to the doctor. After pouring a shot for himself, Peters said, "Want me to get Tayquan? He's waiting upstairs with the rest of the guys, in case you need them."

Taylor took a sip from his glass and studied Bertie thoughtfully.

"No, Jawann. Tell them all to go home. I don't think Mrs. Bigelow will be giving us any more trouble. Besides, I'd like to sit and chat with her a while."

As Jawann Peters lumbered out the door and closed it behind him, Taylor leaned over Bertie and grinned. The smell of his musk-scented cologne was overpowering.

"Now what do you have to say for yourself, Miss High and Mighty?" Roughly, he grabbed the strip of duct tape that covered her mouth and ripped it away in one fluid motion.

"Help!" Bertie screamed. "Help! Someone help me!"

As Bertie continued to scream at the top of her lungs, Taylor sipped his whiskey and studied her silently. When at last she fell silent, the doctor grinned.

"The room is soundproof, my dear. No one but me will hear your pathetic little cries."

"My friends know I'm here." Bertie said. "The police will come looking for me soon." It was a lie, of course, but if Taylor believed her, he might let her go.

"I thoroughly doubt it, my dear. Love your spunk, though. Always have. Almost as much as I hated that do-gooding husband of yours. The day Delroy Bigelow died, I toasted the drunken driver who wiped his sorry ass off this planet." Taylor's face twisted in bitterness.

"Your husband *lectured* me, Bertie. Did you know that? Like I was some delinquent schoolboy. I don't care if he was my lawyer. He had no right to act the way he did. Poking his nose into my private affairs. Taking exception to my business associates. Questioning my authority. Me, Momolu Taylor, the inventor of Testemaxx! Can you imagine?" The doctor's dark eyes sparkled with malice. "I couldn't say anything to him then, of course. But I was determined that one day he would pay for his impudence."

Stunned at the naked hatred playing across the doctor's face, Bertie took a deep breath and gathered her thoughts.

"I'm sure my husband meant no disrespect," she said meekly. "Anyway, it's all in the past, right?"

"So it is, my dear." Taylor chuckled softly. "That is exactly what makes this payback so sweet. I have been looking forward to this moment for a long, long time."

"If you kill me, you'll be caught for sure. Do you really want to spend the rest of your life in jail?"

Even as she made her case, Bertie could tell that her words were not getting through. Momolu Taylor's face glowed with the manic energy of a man who had totally lost touch with reality.

"Hush, my lovely Bertie. Our time together is too short to waste on idle speculation. I have something important to tell you." Taylor drained the rest of his whiskey, stood up, and opened the door. "Get in here, Jawann," he hollered.

Jawann Peters ambled into the room and studied Bertie coldly.

"I told you she'd be trouble," he said. "Tayquan's gone home, but I'll shoot her myself if you want me to."

Like the host of some demented variety show, the doctor bounced cheerfully on the balls of his feet and rubbed his hands together.

"Have a seat, Jawann. Keep a close eye on Mrs. Bigelow here. See that she minds her manners and keeps her mouth shut. I have a little story to tell the two of you."

Peters removed a large handgun from his waistband and shoved it in Bertie's face.

"You heard the man," Peters said. "One wrong word, and I cap you. It would be a pleasure." With an evil grin, he put his gun away and sat down. "Okay, boss," he said. "I don't think you'll be interrupted again. What was it you wanted to say?"

For a long moment no one spoke. Bertie could hear the blood pounding in her ears as she willed herself not to show fear. *Just breathe,* she told herself. *In, out. In, out.* Taylor poured himself a fresh glass of whiskey and positioned his back against the wall across from Bertie and Peters.

After a pregnant silence, he began to speak in a small singsong voice, as though telling a children's story.

"Twenty years ago in Woolworth, Mississippi, there lived a man named Thomas Poundor. Thomas Poundor was a doctor, and one day he got a brilliant idea. He was making a decent income dispensing flu shots and prescribing blood pressure medication and the like. But he realized he could make a lot more money providing the residents of his community with the stuff they really wanted—that little touch of ecstasy that could relieve the tedium and boredom of their everyday lives. I'm talking, of course, about OxyContin. A wonderful drug with a wonderful high. Perfectly legal, as long as it's prescribed by a doctor."

As if reading Bertie's thoughts, Taylor said, "You guessed it, my dear. Doctor Thomas Poundor became a drug dealer. He used the staff and facilities of his little clinic to provide happiness to thousands of blighted souls. It was holy work, really. Too bad his bitchy little wife did not see it that way."

Taylor turned to look at Peters. "I've treated you well, Jawann, have I not?"

"Sure have," Peters said. "You cut me in on your OxyContin hustle. You even gave me free Testemaxx. I can get it on six times a night, if I feel like it."

"Then let me give you a little advice. Never, never, *never* let a woman run your affairs." Taylor took a dainty sip from his glass before resuming his singsong narration.

"Thomas Poundor could have lived happily ever after, running his little clinic and dispensing joy to the populace, except for one thing. He had an uppity, stuck-up, high-yellow bitch of a wife who did not approve of how he made his living. Despite the furs, the Cadillac, the twelve-room mansion, and the swimming pool Poundor gave her, the woman still did not approve."

Like a snake shedding its skin, Taylor abandoned his lilting African accent in favor of a down-home Mississippi drawl.

"The sorry heifer even had the nerve to call the law," he said. "Can you believe that shit? Called the law on her own husband. Her provider. The man who put bread on the table."

The doctor turned to look at Jawann Peters. "Would you ever let a woman tell you how to live, Jawann? Would you?"

Peters's harsh laugh reminded Bertie of a car with a broken fan belt. "I'd a slapped the bitch into next week, boss."

"Dr. Thomas Poundor did better than that," Taylor replied with a grin. "One night, while his wife was fast asleep, he shot her full of Klonopin. The next thing anybody knew, Olivia Poundor was dead, and Thomas Pounder was a free man again. Of course, he had to disappear to Africa for a while afterwards. Change his name and mingle with the natives. But it was a small price to pay for freedom, don't you think?"

Jawann Peters' heavy features wrinkled in confusion. "I don't get it, boss. What's this Poundor guy got to do with it?"

"I *am* Thomas Poundor, you idiot," Momolu Taylor snarled. The doctor's transformation from genial talk show host to raging lunatic was now complete. He was breathing heavily, and his eyes glowed with Messianic fervor. The doctor drained his remaining whiskey in one gulp and hurled his glass to the floor.

"I killed my wife when she attempted to interfere with my operation," he said. "It's been fifteen years since I stuck that lethal needle deep into her tender flesh. In all that time, I haven't forgotten for one moment how sweet it was to watch her die."

Peters nodded impatiently. "It's getting late, boss. When we gonna snuff this broad? I gotta chop her up and dump the pieces in Lake Michigan before the sun comes up."

"All in good time," Taylor said. He took a deep breath. "Before she dies, Mrs. Bigelow must understand fully what a very bad girl she's been. She has been nosing into our affairs, Jawann. Her and that bratty little choirboy LaShawn Thomas." Taylor's voice dripped with scorn. "When LaShawn called Alderman Clark a junkie at the Christmas concert, everyone thought the kid was just running his mouth. But he and I both knew he was talking about the illegal stimulants I was putting in Testemaxx. I knew right away the little shit would have to be eliminated. Didn't I say so, Jawann?"

Jawann Peters grunted. As Bertie watched silently, she could see Peters was unnerved by his boss's sudden descent into madness. He looked uneasily toward the open door and stole a glance at his watch.

Meanwhile, Momolu Taylor was on a roll. He had a captive audience and showed no sign of wrapping up his bizarre harangue.

"That meddlesome judge Theophilous Green was another irritation," he continued. "The old fool really thought I was an African. Can you imagine that? He was going to report me to immigration. If he had, my true identity as Dr. Thomas Poundor might have been discovered. So I had Tayquan steal LaShawn's gun and bring it to me. When I paid Theophilous Green a little visit early New Year's morning, I took the gun with me." Taylor laughed merrily.

"Not a soul saw me slip out of Patrice Soule's apartment and knock on the judge's door, and LeShawn was blamed for the shooting, just as I had planned. I hadn't counted on the kid being released on bail, though. Drive by shootings are not my style, but for a small percentage of my Testemaxx profits, my friends in the Conquering Lions gang were only too happy to help me out."

Momolu Taylor paused and studied Bertie coldly.

"Thought you were pretty clever, didn't you? Contacting the police about our operation. Sticking your nose where it doesn't belong. I tried to warn you. I even sent OJ and Damon to burn down your house, but they failed to complete the job. If you really want something done right, you have to do it yourself."

Taylor grabbed the bottle of whiskey, threw his head back, and took a long swallow.

"Come, Peters. It's time for us to administer Mrs. Bigelow's medication." He pulled on a pair of rubber gloves and extracted a large syringe from the drawer of the desk behind him. "In case you're wondering, Bertie my dear, this is the same lethal injection I gave the lovely Mrs. Poundor fifteen years ago. Hold her head still, Peters. To kill her instantly, I need to hit her right in the carotid artery."

Peters put down his gun and lifted his bulk out of the chair. Even though she knew it was useless, Bertie began to scream at top volume as Peters attempted to hold her head still. Whatever Dr. Momolu Taylor might do to her, she was not going to make it easy.

"Shut up, you crazy bitch," Peters yelled and punched her hard in the face. Stars danced before her eyes as her head slammed back against the table. Syringe in hand, Dr. Taylor loomed over her.

"Quiet, my dear Bertie," the doctor cooed. His face was a twisted mask of hatred. "Do you want me to have Peters shoot you instead? Blow away your pretty face and splatter your brains all over the room? He will, you know. Someone as lovely as you deserves a more poetic end, don't you think?"

Smacking his lips, Momolu Taylor turned to Peters and said, "Revenge is the sweetest drug in the world, Jawann. Let go of Bertie's head. I want to hold her down myself. I want to feel her writhing in agony beneath me as I administer the death blow."

"Sure, boss," Peters muttered. He shrugged and stepped back from the table.

Intent on finding the proper spot to inject the lethal overdose, Momolu Taylor's face was now within inches of Bertie's own. Syringe in hand, the doctor's breath came in ragged gasps as he slowly traced his fingers down her neck.

Bertie gritted her teeth and prepared for the worst. The end was near, and the only possible consolation was that soon she and Delroy would be together once again in heaven. In spite of everything, though, something deep inside Bertie Bigelow was not yet ready to give up. If this loathsome lunatic was going to kill her anyway, she might as well go down fighting. Focused on finding the perfect spot to inject the poison, Taylor relaxed his grip momentarily. Seizing her opportunity, Bertie raised her head and sank her teeth into the doctor's ear until she tasted blood.

Taylor shrieked and dropped to his knees in pain. Blood spurted from his ear and dripped down the side of his neck as the syringe filled with poison clattered to the floor next to him. Peters reached into his pocket for his gun, only to discover he'd set it down on the floor moments before. As he bent down to retrieve his weapon, Bertie heard the sound of feet running in the hallway outside.

"Help!" she screamed, pouring every last ounce of strength she possessed into each syllable. "Help me, someone! Help!"

Seconds later, a half dozen policemen in bulletproof vests waving assault rifles rushed into the room. Jawann Peters stood up slowly, dropped his gun, and raised his arms over his head in surrender.

As the policemen freed Bertie and lifted her off the table, the adrenaline-fueled strength that had sustained her began to slip away. As if by magic, a team of paramedics appeared carrying a stretcher. The last thing Bertie remembered before blacking out completely was the image of Momolu Taylor on his knees, moaning softly and holding his mutilated ear. As blood continued to pour down the doctor's neck, Detective Michael Kulicki walked into the room. He took out a .357 Magnum and pressed it against the doctor's head.

"One wrong move and you're a dead man," the detective said calmly. "The way I'm feeling at the moment, I might just shoot you for the hell of it."

Chapter Thirty-Three

When Bertie regained consciousness, she was lying in a hospital bed with a bandage over one eye and a tube sticking out of her arm.

"Good morning, Mrs. Bigelow. You're a very lucky woman." A brown man in his mid-fifties picked up a clipboard and positioned himself next to her bed. In a lilting Bengali accent, the doctor told Bertie that, had she arrived at Mercy Hospital any later, her sight would have been permanently impaired.

"You have suffered severe physical trauma, including a blow that shattered the bones around your left eye. However, we expect you to make a full recovery. Your karma is good, Mrs. Bigelow," he said. "If you continue to improve, you will be able to return home by the end of the week."

For the next several hours, time as Bertie had been accustomed to living it came to a standstill. Machines monitored her heart rate and tracked her brain waves. Nurses came and went as Bertie slipped in and out of consciousness. When she woke up the next morning, David Mackenzie was standing by her bed with two dozen roses in his hand.

"Is that you, Mac?"

The doctors had removed the bandage from her left eye sometime earlier that day, but her vision was still blurry. The burly lawyer placed the roses on her bedside table and leaned in closer.

"Of course it's me, Bert. I've stopped by a couple of times before, but this is the first time you've been awake. How are you feeling?"

She managed a wan smile. "Better, thanks. They say I'll be out of here by the end of the week."

"You really had me worried," Mac said. "Promise me you'll take better care of yourself." He touched her hand gently. "You mean a lot to me, you know. I'd hate to lose you."

Despite the drugs and the pain in her eye, Bertie felt her pulse quicken. Was Mac trying to tell her something?

"Delroy loved you more than life itself, Bertie. He'd have wanted me to look after you." Mac rubbed his hand absently over the top of his head and sighed. "My wife says I never speak about my feelings. I used to argue with her, but the truth is, she's right. Angelique and I value your friendship, Bertie. I know we've been through some rocky times lately. But I'm determined to make a better effort. A better effort in my marriage, and a better effort with my friends."

Bertie exhaled slowly. Although she hadn't noticed until that moment, she had been holding her breath as Mac spoke. Fortunately, the lighting in her room was dim. With any luck, Mackenzie would not be able to read the disappointment on her face.

"Thanks, Mac. I hardly know what to say."

"No need to say a word," Mac said with a grin. "The minute you get out of here, Angelique and I are taking you out to the finest, most expensive restaurant in Chicago. That's a promise."

Later the same day, Ellen Simpson stopped by the hospital with a plate of goat curry from the Jamaican Jerk Villa. When the nurse on duty expressed concern, Ellen swept past without stopping.

"Mrs. Bigelow is here for her eye," she announced regally. "There's nothing whatsoever wrong with her stomach."

Sure enough, the flavorful stew gave Bertie strength. After a few mouthfuls, she began to feel much more like her usual self.

"Who's your secret admirer?" Ellen said, pointing to the roses on Bertie's bedside table.

"Mac brought them. He's trying to get in touch with his feelings."

"Really?" Ellen winked. "Judging from the cost of roses these days, I'd say the man's got *lots* of feelings."

"Guilty feelings, most likely. He yelled at me for investigating LaShawn's murder. His wife yelled at me on general principle. Mac probably thinks he owes me an apology."

"Two dozen roses' worth? Face it, girlfriend. The man is sweet on you."

"Mind your own business, Ellen. It's really not funny anymore."

Taken aback by Bertie's uncharacteristic display of anger, Ellen bit her lip and remained silent.

"Sorry to yell at you like that," Bertie said in a softer voice. "Mac's not interested in me and never has been. The man is married with a capital 'M.' I don't know why I ever thought things could be any different. I'm just a pathetic, lonely widow, I guess."

"Don't be silly," Ellen said. She leaned forward and squeezed Bertie's hand. "Number one, you are not pathetic. You're beautiful, you are talented, and, most important, you have a warm and caring heart. Any man would be lucky to have you. Number two, you don't need Mac to make you happy. You can make your own happiness. Personally, I plan on giving up men for the foreseeable future."

Bertie put down her fork and sat a little straighter in the bed.

"You don't really mean that, do you?"

"The hell I don't," Ellen said. "They're all dogs, each and every one. Do you know what Mervyn had the nerve to tell me last night?"

"The sexy FBI man?"

"The very same. He says he's not going to see me anymore. Turns out he was just pretending to like me. All he really wanted was to get inside my apartment to look for evidence, to see if I was involved in Raquib's ID scam."

"That's cold," Bertie said. "The man must be part snake."

"Yeah," Ellen said, shaking her head. "Maya Angelou wrote this poem I used to teach in English 101. It's all about the ways a man can shatter you—blow your mind till you never want to feel love again."

"That's probably not the best poem for you right now," Bertie said gently. "Why don't you go with Angelou's 'Phenomenal Woman' instead? That's much more your style."

"I suppose I am pretty phenomenal when I stop to think about it," Ellen said with a wan smile. "Your average woman would not even be capable of getting into a mess like this, let alone surviving it."

"Now you're talking," Bertie said. "Somewhere in all this drama, there's got to be a bright side."

"I've been officially cleared of being involved with Raquib's ID racket. I suppose that's something." Ellen shook her head sadly. "That brother is going down hard, Bertie. When the FBI raided Raquib's place, they found stacks of fake social security cards, passports, and fifty thousand dollars in cash."

"No wonder he was taking you out to all those fancy places," Bertie said, laughing. "He had to do something with all the money he had lying around the house."

"That's one way of looking at it," Ellen said. "Maybe you're right about the 'Phenomenal Woman' thing, Bertie. I'm feeling better already."

"Of course you are. Nothing is going to keep you down for long."

"Got that right. In fact, I think I'll give Jerome a call."

"I thought you'd given up men."

Ellen shrugged. "That was before you brought up 'Phenomenal Woman.' It's only been a couple of weeks. I bet Jerome hasn't forgotten how much fun we had together."

"But didn't you break up with him when you started seeing Raquib?"

"Yes, I did, but gently, Bertie. Gently. I may be a bit gullible where men are concerned, but I know better than to burn all my bridges at once." Ellen grinned. "I was down and out for a minute there, but I'm definitely on my way back. Just like Maya Angelou says—I *rise*, Bertie. I rise!"

Chapter Thirty-Four

Bertie Bigelow was a compulsively punctual person. If she told you she would be somewhere at one o'clock, you could set your watch by it. But on that particular Friday, there was not a parking space to be had for blocks along Prairie Avenue. By the time she walked into Charley Howard's Hot Link Emporium, Bertie was nearly thirty minutes late.

She barely noticed her surroundings as she strode through the crowded restaurant, muttering under her breath and mentally composing her apology. Bertie had nearly reached Ellen's table before she saw that Detective Kulicki, Mrs. Petty, LaShawn's sister, Sherelle, and her son, Benny, were all standing up to greet her. When Dr. Grant and Alderman "Steady Freddy" Clark strolled over to join the group, she was speechless.

"So glad you could make it, Professor Bigelow," Dr. Grant said in his rumbling bass. Smiling broadly, Bertie's boss pulled out a chair and gestured for her to have a seat. "I know you've had a difficult few weeks. Let me be the first to tell you that there is finally some good news coming your way."

As Bertie sat down, Steady Freddie looked pointedly at Dr. Grant and cleared his throat.

"Alderman Clark has something very important to tell you," Grant said. "Let's sit down, shall we?"

Her cheeks flushed with excitement, Bertie looked around the table. Dressed in a brilliant gold-and-red Ghanaian jacket and matching pants, Ellen sat with a self-satisfied grin on her face next to Jerome, the man she'd been dating before Raquib's reappearance. The couple was holding hands and looked very much in love. Next to Jerome, Mrs. Petty, dressed in a black turtleneck, no-nonsense wool cardigan, and a pair of heavy snow pants, monitored the activities of her grandson, Benny, with an eagle eye.

"Hi, Miz Bigelow," the boy said, swinging his legs happily. "Wanna play the singing game with me? The fancy coat man said I should ask you."

"You mean the fancy coat man is here? The one who came to your house after the judge was killed?"

"Sure," Benny said. "That's him right there." The boy lifted a grubby finger and pointed it at Alderman Clark.

In response to the unspoken question in the eyes of the others at the table, Steady Freddy said, "I was starting to suspect Momo had not told me the whole truth about the drugs I was taking. When LaShawn Thomas said what he said at the Christmas concert, I thought he might know something, so I went by his house to speak to him."

"Did you know Judge Green had asked LaShawn to follow you?"

Although the Alderman was not easily flustered, he appeared to stop breathing for a second or two.

"Is that so?" he asked.

"He saw you carry a paper bag out of the Princeton Avenue Natural Health Clinic and hand it to a pair of white guys standing outside."

The alderman burst out laughing. "My, my. That LaShawn Thomas was one busy young man. I can easily resolve that little mystery. The two white men LaShawn saw me talking to were from vice detail. As I mentioned earlier, I was curious what was in the medication I'd been taking. I gave them a bottle so they could check it out for me."

"I'm curious about this medication, as well," Ellen said. She caught Bertie's eye and winked. "Care to tell us what you were being treated for?"

Steady Freddy shot her a dirty look. "I admit to having certain frailties," he said with a bland smile. "But as the great Bruce Lee once said, mistakes are always forgivable, if one has the courage to admit them."

"Amen to that, Brother Clark," Mrs. Petty said, nodding her head. "Jesus will forgive you." She looked pointedly at Ellen, who shrugged and looked away.

Dr. Grant cleared his throat and looked around the table.

"Ladies and gentlemen, we have not come here to dwell on the past. Are you ready, Fred?"

Alderman Clark nodded and stood up.

"The entire community owes you a debt of gratitude for taking on Dr. Taylor and those thugs of his at the Princeton Avenue Natural Health Clinic, Professor Bigelow," he said. "In recognition of your courageous work, the Englewood Businessman's Association has designated you an official Neighborhood Hero." The alderman reached into his briefcase and pulled out a large framed certificate. As he presented it to Bertie, Ellen whipped out a camera and began taking photos.

"One more time, if you please," Dr. Grant said, placing his arm around Bertie's shoulders.

"Does this mean I'm not going to be fired?" Bertie said.

"Fired?" Dr. Grant's portly body shook with laughter. "I wouldn't dream of firing our very own Neighborhood Hero."

At that moment, the doors to the kitchen swung open and Charley Howard, dressed in a grease-stained apron, a pair of denim overalls, and a battered straw hat, approached their table carrying a bottle of Champagne.

"Party time, folks," the Hot Sauce King hollered as he splashed a generous shot of Champagne into each person's glass. "Let the good times roll!"

"You're a prince, Charley," Bertie said. "I hope you'll forgive me for all those terrible things I said about you before."

Howard waved his meaty fist in the air dismissively. "It's all water under the bridge, darlin'. And in the spirit of forgiveness, I've decided to drop my libel suit. I can't afford to be holdin' grudges against someone I might run into at the next Octagon function, can I?"

"Thanks, Charley," Bertie said. "Now that the real killer is safely behind bars, can I ask you one more question? What really happened between you and LaShawn Thomas the night he came to see you?"

"The kid wanted protection," Howard said. "He knew the Lions were after him, and he thought maybe I could get Tony Roselli to help him out." The Hot Sauce King paused and looked Bertie in the eye. "What the kid didn't know is that the Rosellis and I are quits. When I found out I was now a member of the Octagon Society, I sat down with the old man himself. We worked out an arrangement." Howard wiped his hands on his apron. "I couldn't have helped the kid, even if I wanted to."

"After he met with Charley Howard, LaShawn stole a box of isopropyl nitrite from the clinic," Detective Kulicki said. "He intended to take the box to the police, but the Lions got to him first."

"But how did you know I'd been kidnapped?" Bertie said.

Kulicki grinned and nodded in Ellen's direction. "Do you want to tell her, or shall I?"

"I've got this one, Detective." Jerome Howell put his arm around Ellen's shoulders and pulled her close. "Your rescue was entirely due to this brilliant and beautiful woman right here," he said proudly.

"When you didn't call me first thing the next morning like you promised, I got worried. And when you didn't show up for your Music History class, I knew something was wrong. I didn't want to get you in trouble with Doctor Grant, so I decided to look into things myself. I, um, made some calls," Ellen said.

When she hesitated, Jerome kissed her cheek. "It's alright, baby. I don't mind. It's all in the rearview at this point."

"I had a friend at the FBI," Ellen said, blushing. "When he refused to look for you, I nearly dumped his useless behind right there and then. I was one angry black woman. I had a gut feeling something was not right."

"She called my private line. Then she called my precinct captain. And *then* she called Commissioner Bailey," Kulicki said, laughing. "I don't know what she said, but it must have been something amazing. Next thing I know, my boss is calling me at home."

"She cussed those folks six ways to Sunday until somebody finally got Detective Kulicki on the line," Jerome said proudly. "Once he figured out what was going on, he was able to trace GPS on your cell phone right to the Princeton Avenue Clinic."

As a team of waiters arrived and began distributing steaming platters of BBQ ribs, candied yams, and collard greens, Alderman Clark looked at his Rolex and got to his feet.

"Sorry to miss out on such magnificent soul food, but I've got a campaign rally on the other side of town," he said. "Patrice Soule is going to perform. If the spirit moves me, I might even sing a number myself. Would you like to join us, Bertie? You could sing a song, perhaps make a small speech?"

Bertie smiled and shook her head, "Not tonight, Alderman. Perhaps some other time. Give Miss Soule my regards, though."

"Professor Bigelow will be far too busy at Metro College to be making campaign appearances," Dr. Grant chimed in. He stood up and put on his coat. "Unless, of course, your office intends to compensate the college for her valuable time?"

Steady Freddy Clark smiled knowingly. "Can I have my driver drop you somewhere, Humbert?" He draped his cashmere coat over his arm and nodded goodbye. "We can discuss this further on the way downtown. I am sure we'll be able to reach some kind of understanding."

As the two men walked side by side out of the restaurant, Ellen giggled wickedly.

"Well, Miss Neighborhood Hero," she said, "if I were you, I'd be asking our Fearless Leader for a raise about now."

When the laughter at the table subsided, Detective Kulicki studied Bertie thoughtfully.

"I underestimated both your intelligence and your courage, Mrs. Bigelow. If you ever decide to change careers, you'd make a great private detective."

Bertie blushed at the unexpected compliment and ducked her head.

"I have to say, it was kind of exciting," she said, spearing a candied yam with her fork. "Not that I anticipate doing this kind of thing again."

Ellen poked Bertie playfully in the ribs. "Keep an open mind, Miss Neighborhood Hero," she said. "You never know what fate has in store."

~ Fini ~

About Carolyn Wilkins

 Carolyn Wilkins is a Professor of Ensembles at Berklee College of Music and the author of *They Raised Me Up: A Black Single Mother and the Women Who Inspired Her, Damn Near White: An African American Family's Rise from Slavery to Bittersweet Success* and *Tips for Singers: Performing, Auditioning, Rehearsing.*

An accomplished jazz pianist, composer, and vocalist, Carolyn's performance experience includes radio and television appearances with her group SpiritJazz, a concert tour of South America as a Jazz Ambassador for the US State Department, performances with the Pittsburgh Symphony as a percussionist under Andre Previn, and shows featuring Melba Moore, Nancy Wilson, and the Fifth Dimension. Born and raised on the South Side of Chicago, Carolyn now lives in Cambridge, Massachusetts.

Made in the USA
Charleston, SC
23 January 2016